EVIL WOMAN

JULIE MULHERN

J&M PRESS

ACKNOWLEDGMENTS

It takes a village to write a book. To Sally Berneathy, Kathie McLean Roper, and Matt, thank you. A million times over!

PRAISE FOR THE COUNTRY CLUB MURDERS

"Set in Kansas City, Missouri, in 1974, this cozy mystery effectively recreates the era through the details of down-to-earth Ellison's everyday life."

– Booklist

"There's no way a lover of suspense could turn this book down because it's that much fun."

– Suspense Magazine

"What a fun read! Murder in the days before cell phones, the internet, DNA and AFIS."

– Books for Avid Readers

"Mulhern nails the fierce fraught mother-daughter relationship, fearlessly tackles what hides behind the Country Club façade, and serves up justice in bombshell fashion. A truly satisfying slightly twisted cozy."

– Gretchen Archer, *USA Today* Bestselling Author of the Davis Way Crime Capers

"Mulhern continues to depict the trappings of a privileged community...that blends a strong mystery with the demands of living in an exclusive society. Watching Ellison develop the strength of character to break through both her own and her society's expectations is a sheer delight."

– *Kings River Life Magazine*

"Mulhern's lively, witty sequel to *The Deep End* finds Kansas City, Mo., socialite Ellison Russell reluctantly attending a high school football game...Cozy fans will eagerly await Ellison's further adventures."

– *Publishers Weekly*

"What a fun read! Murder in the days before cell phones, the internet, DNA and AFIS."

– *Books for Avid Readers*

"An enjoyable, frequently amusing mystery with a mixture of off-beat characters that create twists and turns to keep Ellison— and the reader—off-guard while trying to solve the murder and keep herself out of jail. The plot is well-structured and the characters drawn with a deft hand. Setting the story in the mid-1970s is an inspired touch...A fine start to this mystery series, one that is highly recommended."

– *Mysterious Reviews*

CHAPTER ONE

June, 1975
Kansas City, Missouri

I stumbled into the kitchen, spotted Mr. Coffee's near full pot, and offered him a grateful smile. "I missed you." More than words could say.

He preened and sat taller on the counter. *Welcome home. How was Italy?*

"Fabulous. Magical. Best trip ever. Except for the coffee. Cappuccino is good, but try ordering one after ten o'clock in the morning. If the waiter deigns to serve you, he does it with a sneer. Italians drink espresso after ten. It's too strong, and I can't wrap my hands around a demi-tasse." I took a mug from the cabinet and wrapped my fingers around it.

Well, you're home now. How are you feeling? Jet lag? Mr. Coffee was always so concerned with my well-being.

"A bit. It never lasts long. Right now, I need coffee." I poured dark brown nectar into the mug and added cream.

Ellison—

I held up a finger. "Just a minute." Some might think it odd I had a first-name relationship with my coffee maker, but during my first marriage, Mr. Coffee was the man on whom I depended. "There's nothing like the first sip."

Ellison—

Whatever he wanted to tell me would keep for ten seconds. I raised the cup to my lips, took a large sip, and sprayed bitter, cold coffee across the counter.

To his credit, Mr. Coffee didn't laugh. But he did observe a highly suspicious silence.

I took those seconds to blot coffee from the front of my robe. "Are you broken?" A hint of hysteria tinged my voice. "Is there a Mr. Coffee fixer? Maybe that dishwasher repairman from TV can fix you, the one who complains he has nothing to do."

I'm not broken.

Thank God. "Then why is the coffee cold?"

Your new husband pushed my button hours ago.

Anarchy did this to me? The honeymoon was over. "And?"

My burner goes cool after two hours.

Anarchy hadn't realized I'd sleep so late. Even so, he could have emptied the pot, refilled the reservoir, and added grounds. I did all those things now. Then I pushed Mr. Coffee's button.

While the coffee brewed, I wiped down the kitchen counter. "Did we miss much while we were gone?"

Not here. Mr. Coffee, with his yellow gingham face and access to endless caffeine, had a naturally sunny nature, but he sounded almost snarky.

"Boring without me?"

Dull as decaf.

"Dull can be good." Dull meant I didn't find any bodies. Dull meant no one tried to kill me.

Dull is dull.

"Dull is restful."

If you say so. He didn't agree but refused to argue with me. I loved that about him.

Ding, dong.

I glanced toward the front hall. "Libba or Mother?"

Your mother wouldn't bother with the bell.

"True." I gathered the folds of my soiled bathrobe, tightened its belt, and stared longingly at Mr. Coffee's near full pot.

Answer the door. The coffee will be ready in minutes.

Ding, dong.

Max, our Weimaraner with plans for world domination, lifted his head from his paws. He was peeved. With me. I'd left him at home. If I'd taken him to Italy, he might have conquered the Veneto. Or Rome.

Ding, dong.

"I'm coming," I muttered.

Max joined me in the hallway. His stubby tail even wagged.

"Am I forgiven?"

He lifted his doggy nose and trotted past me. Not forgiven. Not even close. Forgiveness would cost me doggy treats, extra walks, and an hour-long scratch behind his silky ears.

I yanked the door open.

"Oh, good. You're awake."

I stared at my best friend. "Do you have any idea what time it is?"

"Do you?"

I didn't. "We got home at two this morning." After a full day of travel.

She peered over my shoulder. "Is Anarchy still sleeping?"

"Anarchy got up early and went to the station."

My conscience twinged. I couldn't hold cold coffee against him. Not when he was at his desk while I slept.

"And Grace? Where's Grace?"

My daughter had padded downstairs when we arrived home,

offered us sleepy hugs, and explained her exhausting schedule. Two-a-days for swim team, plus an extra hour of laps if she wanted a spot as an A swimmer, then babysitting for a toddler who never slowed down. She'd hear about Italy later.

Dead on my feet, I'd promised the extra suitcase we'd picked up in Florence held multiple surprises, then toddled off to bed.

"She's at swim team."

Libba pushed into the foyer and wrapped me in a warm hug. "I missed you. Tell me everything."

"We shopped, we ate good food, we drank great wine, and we looked at great art."

"That cobbler's shop in Milan?"

When I mentioned great art, I meant Michelangelo's David. But the cobbler was also an artist. "There's a slight chance I went a bit overboard." But a woman could never own too many boots (even if she had to wait till autumn to wear them).

"What else?"

"We wandered lemon groves."

Libba rolled her eyes. "You got out of bed for lemons? Anarchy's doing something wrong. Or you are." Her grin was especially naughty. "Tell me, and we'll figure it out."

Libba was not getting bedroom details. "We watched the sunset from the patio of a Tuscan villa."

"If our places were reversed, I'd tell you everything."

And I'd plug my ears. "Not that I'd want to hear it."

She pouted. "You're no fun."

"But you missed me despite my stick-in-the-mud ways." I led her to the kitchen, poured her a cup of coffee, and at long last filled my mug. "What happened while I was gone?"

"Prudence Davies' mother is dead."

"I figured she'd make it to one-hundred. Mean women live forever. What happened?"

A knowing smile curled Libba's lips. "There's a rumor."

"About?"

"Muriel didn't die of natural causes."

"Who killed her?" My mind settled on the obvious suspect. "Prudence?"

"Who else?"

Prudence, a killer? Really? I closed my eyes and considered. No one would blame Prudence for killing her mother. Muriel ranked among the most unpleasant people I'd ever met. And I included in that count numerous murderers and Prudence, who'd had a torrid affair with my late husband. "Is there an investigation?"

Libba nodded. "You know what this means?"

"Prudence may go to prison." I didn't pretend sadness. I barely refrained from dancing a jig (but only because I might spill my coffee).

"Nope. Well, yes. More importantly, someone in our circle died, and you didn't swim into, trip over, or even discover the body."

I had a deplorable habit of finding the newly dead.

The back door opened, and Aggie, the woman who took care of me and my daughter Grace (and now Anarchy), bustled into the kitchen. She carried two grocery bags and wore an orange kaftan with turquoise flowers. The hem and the cuffs sported turquoise pompoms. She smiled when she saw us. "You're up."

I took a bag from her arms and set it on the counter. "I'm up."

"Should I make fresh coffee?"

"I just made a pot."

"I should have started a new one before I left."

Libba frowned at us. "What's the problem?"

"Mrs. Jones likes to come downstairs to hot coffee."

"And?"

"And this morning I came down to a cold pot."

Aggie and Mr. Coffee winced. Libba rubbed the pad of her

thumb over her bent pointer finger. The world's saddest song, on the world's smallest violin.

"It's a little thing. Anarchy and I will work it out. He can refill the grounds and reservoir mornings when he leaves early." I tightened my hold on my coffee mug. We'd been home less than twelve hours, and already there was a hiccup. Marriage was going to be an adjustment. For both of us. I pulled a bottle of cream from the grocery bag and put it in the fridge. "Libba just told me Prudence Davies is a suspect in her mother's murder."

"How did she die?" asked Aggie. A question I should have asked.

"Suffocated."

"How awful." Aggie took celery stalks from the sack and put them next to the sink for washing.

Libba flashed a ghoulish grin. "Would you expect anything less than awful from Prudence?"

Aggie chuckled. "Good point. Are there any other suspects?" She pulled a box of raisin bran from the sack.

I pointed at the box. "What's that?"

Aggie glanced at the cereal in her hand, and her brow creased, as if I'd asked a trick question. "Raisin bran."

"I see that. Why is it in my house?"

"Detective Jones likes raisin bran."

"He does? I married a man who eats raisins? You're sure?"

Aggie covered her mouth with her hand as if she were hiding a smile. "When I told him I was marketing today, he asked me to buy some."

I grabbed the counter and lowered myself to a stool. "Raisins?"

"Ellison hates raisins." Libba grinned as if she found raisins amusing. "She hates them with a passion most people reserve for their arch-enemies."

"Take a perfectly good grape and let it shrivel and rot."

Aggie frowned. "Rot might be a bit strong."

I cut off Aggie's raisin defense with a wave of my hand. "They're infested with insect eggs."

"That's not true," said Libba.

"It is," I insisted. "I read it in the paper. Raisins are awful." And they'd soon be on a shelf in my pantry.

Libba chuckled. "First, your new husband drank your coffee, then he asked for raisins. What's next? Grapes in the chicken salad?"

I glanced at the celery, then skewered Aggie with a severe look (so she knew I meant business). "That is my line in the sand. Grapes do not belong in chicken salad."

"I'm sure Aggie could dice them—"

I turned my look on Libba. "Don't you have someplace else to be?"

"Nope." She popped the "p" and grinned. "What did you bring me from Italy?"

"You don't deserve a gift."

She stuck out her tongue. "Of course I do. Is it something good?"

I'd been looking forward to giving Libba and Aggie their gifts, but I pretended reluctance (they were part of the raisin conspiracy). "Fine. You two stay here. I'll be right back." I ran up the back stairs and dashed into the blue guest bedroom where Anarchy and I had left our bulging suitcases. I rifled through four before I found the scarf box that held Libba's gift and the bag that held Aggie's. I grabbed both and returned to the kitchen.

Libba's gaze landed on the box, and she rubbed her hands together. "Is that what I think it is?"

"I don't know." It was.

I handed over the box, and she ripped off the top. Her eager fingers ripped through the logoed tissue paper, and she pulled the silk twill scarf from its box. "It's gorgeous. Thank you."

"You're welcome. The saleswoman promised that pattern is not yet available in America." I handed the bag to Aggie. "I hope you like it."

She pulled out a kaftan in a geometric Pucci print in harvest gold, cream, brown, burnt sienna, and avocado. The slightly fitted sleeves ended above the elbow and were finished with twelve inches of harvest gold fringe. Her smile wobbled, and she stroked the fabric. "It's beautiful. Too pretty to wear."

"Don't be silly," said Libba. "Mac will love you in that." Mac was Aggie's boyfriend and the owner of a delicatessen and catering company.

Pink touched Aggie's cheeks, and she held up the new kaftan so its vibrant fabric covered her orange and turquoise. "You think?"

"I'm sure of it," Libba replied.

"Thank you, Ellison."

"You're welcome. I'm glad you like it." I stood and refilled my coffee mug.

"Should I make another pot?"

Such a silly question. "Please."

Brnng, brnng.

We all stared at the phone as if it had just grown horns and hefted a pitchfork, but only I spoke. "Mother?"

"Chances are good." Libba's voice had a laissez-faire quality that put me on edge.

Aggie picked up the receiver. "Jones residence. I'm sorry she's not available. Yes, she's home. She arrived early this morn-ing. I'll let her know you called." She winced and hung up.

"Mother?" I asked. If so, Aggie deserved a raise.

"No." Aggie shook her head, and her orange curls bounced like springs. "I thought you might want more coffee before you spoke with her."

"With whom?"

"Prudence Davies."

Libba narrowed her eyes and tapped a finger on her pursed lips. "Gee, I wonder what she wants."

"You don't think she'd call me for help?"

"Yes," Libba and Aggie spoke in unison.

"She hates me." For reasons known only to Prudence, she behaved as if I'd infringed on her relationship with Henry. As if she were the injured party.

Libba snorted. "The woman is desperate, and you're married to a homicide detective."

Had Prudence truly committed matricide? If so, why? Sure, I'd considered murdering Mother—especially when she pushed me toward Hunter Tafft, a lawyer who'd shown an interest after my late husband's murder. But, at the end of the day, I loved her. Mother—more than anyone—was in my corner. "Tell me what happened."

"It happened last weekend." Libba slid a stack of mail across the counter and scrutinized a catalog cover.

"At Muriel's house?" Prudence lived with her mother a few blocks from me.

"Yes." She rejected the catalog and flipped through my unopened mail.

"Was anyone else at home?"

"No."

"And Muriel was definitely suffocated?"

"That's what Jinx says." Our friend Jinx was a world-class gossip who seldom got her facts wrong.

Libba held up a large blue envelope. "Are you going?"

"What is it?"

She handed over the envelope addressed to Mr. and Mrs. Anarchy Jones. "Sarah and August Elmhurst are having a cocktail party. Are you going?"

"I don't know when it is or if Anarchy's available," I hedged. On the one hand, this was the first invitation addressed to both me and Anarchy. On the other, it was a party at Sarah's. I liked

Sarah, but she didn't eat. No one had witnessed a bite of food crossing her lips in six years. Well, aside from the olives in her martinis. And, because she didn't actually eat, the food at her parties was abysmal. Cocktail weenies, meatballs in a God-awful goop made from grape jelly and chili sauce, and Polynesian kabobs (sausage, pineapple, and water chestnuts marinated in honey and soy sauce). "I'll ask him."

"We could go to dinner beforehand," Libba suggested.

I grabbed a knife from the drawer, slit open the invitation, and frowned. "It's this Saturday."

"It'll be fun. Dinner, I mean. I haven't had Chinese in ages. We'll go to that place on the Plaza."

House of Toy? Tempting. But there was no way she'd pressure me into attending this party. Not until Anarchy understood the ramifications of inedible food and generous pours of expensive liquor. Rather than argue, I changed the subject. "I'm guessing things are still going well with Charlie?" Libba had recently taken up with my newly divorced next-door neighbor.

"Yes." She pulled at the collar of her blouse. "Back to Prudence. Do you think she has it in her to commit murder?"

Apparently, two could change the subject. "She had the opportunity, they lived in the same house. Also, it's Prudence. She's a terrible person. And then there's Muriel. That Prudence didn't kill her mother before now is a miracle."

Libba opened a catalog. "So that's it?"

"What do you mean?"

"You won't investigate?"

I frowned. "Me?"

She looked up from a page filled with dresses. "You."

"I didn't like Muriel. I don't like Prudence. For once, I didn't find the body. And it's none of my business."

"That's a no?"

"That's a no." Probably.

"Was the house locked for the night?" asked Aggie.

"Yes." Libba tapped a blue linen dress with a lacquered nail. "But Jinx says their hidden key is missing."

"Hidden under a flowerpot?" I asked.

"Worse. Under the welcome mat."

I'd given up hiding a key outside when a killer used it to enter my house. "Aggie, did you have house keys made for Anarchy?"

"He took them with him this morning."

"Thank you."

Libba dog-eared my catalog, then picked up a bright pink envelope. "You're invited to the Dawsons' couple's shower for Summer Hagewood and her fiancé."

"It's nice having you here. I don't have to open my mail."

"Not my fault we're invited to the same parties."

"What was the time of death?" I asked.

Libba smirked. "How's not investigating going?"

Brnng, brnng.

Aggie reached for the phone, and I topped off my coffee mug then held up the pot.

Libba covered her mug with her palm.

"Jones' residence." Aggie placed her pointer finger on her lips, and Libba and I fell silent.

"Good morning, Mrs. Walford. No. I'm sorry she's not up yet." Aggie paled. "Yes, Libba is here. She's having coffee and waiting for Mrs. Jones to wake up." Aggie's face tightened as if Mother had imparted terrible news, then she nodded. "I'll tell her."

No one uttered a sound until the receiver was safely back in its cradle.

"How did Frances know I was here?" Libba demanded. "Is she psychic?"

"Marian Dixon," I replied. It was a safe guess. My across-the-street neighbor was always nosy, but since I started finding bodies, watching my house had become her favorite hobby.

"And she reports to your mother?"

I gave a grim nod. "At least once a day. More often if anything interesting happens. What does Mother want, Aggie?"

"You're to call her, and she expects you, Detective Jones, and Grace for dinner."

I resisted burying my head in my hands. "Tonight?"

Aggie's face tightened in an apologetic grimace. "Don't shoot the messenger."

"Look on the bright side," said Libba.

"There's a bright side?" I couldn't see one.

"She can't be mad at you for finding Muriel's body."

"You developed a sense of humor while I was gone?"

CHAPTER TWO

The sun was perfect, and the pool deck smelled of coconut suntan lotion, chlorine, and heat.

I closed my eyes behind my sunglasses and considered a nap.

In the pool, children splashed, boys played gutter-ball, and every so often a lifeguard blew his whistle and yelled at an intrepid youngster to stay off the lane ropes. At regular intervals, the lifeguard at the towel desk called a teenager to the telephone. The noises were familiar. Even soothing.

Three girls, perhaps a year younger than Grace, lounged in chairs fifteen feet from mine. Their skin glistened with baby oil and iodine, and they chattered about David Cassidy, the latest issue of a teen magazine, and how many limes they liked in their Tabs.

A contented sigh slipped past my lips. A thousand chores waited for me at home. Unpack. Return umpteen phone messages. Reply to six invitations. Pay bills. Call Jinx and get the skinny on Prudence. But after calling Mother and telling her we could not come to dinner (she was not pleased), I'd turned my back on my to-do list and escaped to the pool. This afternoon, a chaise lounge next to glistening water was exactly what I needed.

"Ellison?"

I turned my head, opened my eyes, and reconsidered my choices.

Sarah Elmhurst, who wore a tiny bikini, smiled down at me. "May I join you?" Without waiting for an answer, she dropped a pool bag onto the chaise next to mine and put her iced tea on the table between us. "When did you get back from Italy?"

"Early this morning." And I wanted time to relax and recharge without making conversation. Also, I'd eaten my way through Italy, and now a woman so thin she didn't cast a shadow sat next to me. I sucked in my tummy.

"Was Italy marvelous? I've never been. August and I bought a house in Vail when Weston was little." She pulled a bottle of suntan oil from her bag. "It seemed like a fine idea, but August insists we go there every vacation. I love the mountains. I do. But visiting a beach or taking a trip to Europe wouldn't kill us. Anyhoo. Marvelous?" She meant Italy.

"Yes."

She angled the chaise so she'd get full sun, unfurled a beach towel, then stretched out. "You must be exhausted."

I covered a yawn. "A bit tired."

"Did you hear about Muriel Jarrett?" Her stage whisper was audible to the whole pool deck, and heads turned.

"I did. So awful."

Sarah rubbed oil into skin that was already deeply tanned. "I wonder if Prudence will be arrested soon."

I could sense ears straining to hear my reply. Even the teenage girls, who'd engaged in a spirited argument about which Cassidy brother was better looking, fell silent. "I haven't the slightest."

Sarah's nose wrinkled as if I'd disappointed her. "You seem very blasé. I thought you'd be dancing or breaking into song."

Did she think we lived in a Broadway musical? True, I'd experienced a schadenfreude moment when Libba told me about Prudence's troubles, but I'd moved past the desire to jig. "Muriel is dead."

She batted away my point with a wave of her manicured fingers. "The woman was as mean as a snake."

Even if I'd had the energy to argue, Sarah made a good point. But I'd given the matter some thought (the drive from my house to the club) and I couldn't quite see Prudence as a killer. "I can't imagine Prudence murdered her mother." My own mother had provided me with numerous motives for murder, but I'd only considered killing her once or twice…and thinking and doing were very different things.

Relationships between mothers and daughters were tricky. Even fraught. Mothers saw their daughters as reflections of themselves. Daughters looked for criticism in compliments. Whenever Mother told me my hair looked nice, I assumed it was time for a trim.

I spent decades living under Mother's thumb. I might still be there, but my first husband's death had served as a wake-up call. Did I want to live the life she chose for me, or the one I wanted? I'd done the impossible. I'd made a stand and married the man I loved. She'd fought that decision till the moment Anarchy and I exchanged vows. But, now that we were married, she accepted my new husband (at least I hoped she did) and she'd tempered her demands. Yes, she still expected command performance dinners, regular phone calls, the occasional Sunday brunch, and my adherence to the rules of polite society as she understood them, but those were small directives, easily managed or ignored.

"Didn't Prudence have an affair with your husband?"

Sarah's question put thoughts of Mother clean out of my head and had me lifting my brows above the rims of my glasses. Sarah knew the answer to that question. Why was she asking?

"With my late husband. Not the man I just married." The man who'd investigated my first husband's death.

"That's who I meant. Henry. It had to hurt. Henry and Prudence."

"Yes." And I so enjoyed it when people poked the scar. I glanced at my iced tea glass (sadly still full, I couldn't escape to the snack bar for a refill).

"What was he thinking? You're a lovely woman. And Prudence? She'd lose a beauty contest with Mr. Ed."

What was Sarah's angle? Was her reminder of past sins a way to get me talking? I did not like Prudence. At all. But that didn't mean I'd kick her when she was down. "What else happened while I was gone?"

Sarah's brow wrinkled, and she crossed her arms beneath her substantial cleavage. I hadn't taken the bait, and she was not pleased.

"Surely something else happened," I insisted. "Something scandalous?" There was always a scandal brewing.

Sarah huffed. "The custody battle between Sabra and the Tiki bartender got ugly."

I blinked. "Pardon?"

"You haven't heard?" Sarah glanced left and right, presumably looking for eavesdroppers. Finding none, she said, "Sabra Davidson went to college in Florida, met some bartender, and married him. Shirley and Dan were beside themselves, but they told no one. Anyhoo, Sabra got pregnant, had a baby, and then the marriage fell apart. Of course it did. What did the girl expect? That a bartender could keep her in Lilly Pulitzer shifts and Bernardo sandals?" Sarah shook her head at the foolish dreams of youth. "After a few months lived in poverty, Sabra gathered up her son and came home. Well, the bartender followed her up here."

"How awful." How had Shirley and Dan kept this quiet for so long? "What happened?"

"The Davidsons hired a private investigator to investigate him. I haven't heard what they found, but I do know the bartender is demanding joint custody and insists that Sabra return to Florida."

I wasn't terribly worried about Sabra. Her parents could afford the best lawyers. "What a mess."

"It is," Sarah agreed. "I can't imagine how difficult this must be for poor Shirley. Tell me about your trip. Did you taste lots of good wine?"

"We did. And we ate amazing food."

She wrinkled her nose at the mention of sustenance. Sarah was a woman convinced she'd hold on to her youth if she held on to her waistline. Her slender body, perky breasts (consensus around the bridge table was she'd had them done) and carefully highlighted hair couldn't hide the truth. Her twenties were a distant memory. Her thirties were fading fast. And her forties were halfway over. "Did you meet any interesting people?"

"One. We were sitting at a café in Milan, and Anarchy was reading the paper—"

"Anarchy reads Italian?"

"The International Herald Tribune," I clarified. "We were drinking coffee, Anarchy was reading, and I was sketching when a man approached us."

"A movie star?"

I rolled my eyes behind the cover of my sunglasses. "A gallery owner. He'd spotted my sketch and liked it. We ended up having dinner with him and his wife. They were charming. It wasn't until later I realized who he was."

"Are gallery owners famous?"

"Some are. He is. Lloyd Foster's gallery is one of the most important in London."

"Well, that's nice." Her voice was flat. Clearly, she'd been hoping for a story about Marcello Mastroianni or Franco Nero or Sophia Loren. "I always say, a woman needs a hobby."

That was rich coming from a woman whose hobby was counting calories. "Art is more of a career."

She patted my hand. "Of course it is. That's why you're at the pool on a Tuesday afternoon and not in your studio."

That Sarah had a point (a small one) made her even more annoying.

I forced a smile. "That's the wonderful thing about being my own boss. I can take a day off whenever I want."

"Aren't you just back from a two-week vacation?"

"I am. With a sketchbook full of ideas. I never know when something—a vista, a person, a street—will trigger an emotional response. When that happens, I make a sketch. There's a pad in my pool bag now." If she wasn't careful, I'd sketch her as a size eight. Maybe a ten.

"That reminds me. I'm chairing an auction this fall. Will you donate a canvas?"

"You just called me a hobbyist."

She winced. "You took it the wrong way. I had no idea you took your art so seriously."

If I ate nothing but beef bouillon and gin-soaked olives, I might be as obtuse as Sarah. No, not obtuse. I'd be impossible. "Let's go to lunch and discuss it."

A frown creased her forehead. "I don't eat lunch." Was she worried her husband might trade her in for a newer, skinnier model? It happened to loads of women. Women who went from sipping iced tea poolside to spritzing perfume on unsuspecting shoppers. "Can't we discuss it now?"

"I've been home less than a day, have a show coming up in Chicago, and need to inventory the canvases in my studio. I can't promise you anything today."

She pouted. "But—"

"Ellison! You're back. Why didn't you call me?" Jinx, who wore tennis whites, planted her hands on her hips and glared at me as if I were Missy Crandall, her partner who double faulted to lose the last set in the club championship. Sarah, she ignored.

"We arrived this morning."

"And my phone didn't ring."

"Next time I get home at two in the morning, I'll call you."

"You heard about Muriel Jarrett?"

"Yes."

"And?" She eyed me expectantly.

"You know more than I do."

"She was suffocated."

"So I'm told."

She tilted her head. "Anarchy told you?"

"Libba. And she says you told her."

Jinx frowned as if I'd presented her with bad news. As if she hoped for additional sources of information (like a homicide detective). "I heard the killer used a bed pillow. Murdered her in her sleep." Jinx drew out "sleep," making a statement into a question.

"Jinx, I truly know nothing."

She tapped her pursed lips with her pointer finger, and her eyes looked into the distance.

"Anarchy left for work before I heard about the murder. I haven't spoken to him."

She returned her gaze to me. "I wonder, did Muriel wake up?"

If so, the pressure of a pillow held to her face, the inability to breathe, the impossible task of fighting a younger and stronger assailant (younger and stronger were a safe assumption; Muriel had been older than dirt) must have been terrifying.

"Ask your husband." *Then, tell me what he says* was unspoken.

If Anarchy shared anything with me and asked me to keep quiet, I wouldn't tell Jinx. Nor anyone else. I offered her a bland smile.

"Hmph." She scowled as if she sensed my new-found commitment to discretion. "You've heard about Sabra?"

"Sarah just told me."

Jinx shifted her gaze and offered Sarah a miniscule nod. "What about Elizabeth and Wes Lynn?"

Elizabeth and Wes were younger than us by ten years. But Elizabeth sat on three committees at the club, was active in the Junior League, and played decent golf, good tennis, and a mean game of bridge. We liked her. "What about them?"

"They adopted a baby."

"That's wonderful news."

Jinx's gaze flitted to Sarah then returned to me. "I'll tell you more later. How was Italy?"

"*Favolosa.*"

"Did you see anything but the inside of hotel rooms?"

Next to me, Sarah choked on her tea.

"Shops, galleries, museums, cafés, restaurants, churches...I could go on."

"Ellison met a gallery owner," said Sarah.

"Did you?" Jinx's tone was blatantly disinterested.

"Lloyd Foster," I told her. "He runs a gallery in London."

She perked up. "Does that mean a show in England?"

"Not this year." I wasn't near ready for my show in Chicago. In retrospect, I should have spent the day in my studio instead of the pool. Spreading paint on a canvas was far more relaxing than fielding questions about a murder case.

"You'll be at bridge tomorrow?" Jinx asked.

"Wouldn't miss it."

"It's a home meet, but we'll arrive long before the swimmers."

"A home meet?"

"Problem?"

"Yes. I declined Mother's dinner invitation for tonight and told her we'd come tomorrow. But Grace will be swimming."

Swim meets began at four, lasted for hours, and finished with a buffet supper. There was no way we could join Mother and Daddy for dinner. I needed to call her as soon as possible.

She grimaced on my behalf. "We'll talk at bridge." She turned on her heel and left without having actually spoken to Sarah.

"You're at odds?" I asked. Jinx had never liked Sarah, but this was the first time she'd been openly rude.

"She got a story wrong. I called a lawyer."

Jinx? Wrong? "What story?" I waited for her to explain, but Sarah's lips were a thin line, and a deep crease cut through her forehead. Whatever the story, she wasn't telling.

I made a note to ask about Sarah's story when I saw Jinx. "How's Weston? Is he keeping busy this summer?" Weston, Sarah and August's son, had just finished his freshman year at college.

"He's working at the company." August manufactured a part that was essential to the running of cars. "Learning the business."

"Has he declared a major?"

"Business. With a minor in theatre." Chances were excellent that Weston, if left to his own devices, would have majored in the theatre. But, as an only child, he was expected to take over his father's business.

"August must be thrilled."

Sarah wrinkled her nose. "August thinks Weston should switch his minor to engineering, but the poor boy got my math skills, which are non-existent."

Had August lost his mind? His son won the lead in every play in high school, had even starred in summer productions in the park. The young man had less chance of becoming an engineer than I did. "Is he dating anyone?"

"If so, he doesn't tell his mother. What about Grace? Is she working this summer?"

"Swim team and babysitting."

"I bet she's glad you're home."

Missing my daughter was the only wrinkle in a smooth trip. "I'm glad to be home."

"How is your new husband settling in?"

"We're swinging by his old apartment tonight to pick up his things." Thus far, Anarchy had moved his clothes into a closet at my house. We needed to make my house our house. And moving his belongings seemed the best way to accomplish that goal. "Also, he has a cat." Anarchy's partner, Peters, kept the feline while we traveled, but now that we were back in town, there was no reason not to move the cat to our home. No reason but Max's deep and abiding dislike of cats. I feared for our house.

Especially since I knew first-hand the chaos Max and McCallester could wreak. Grace—without my permission—had rescued the cat and snuck him into the house. In short order, McCallester and Max had destroyed a chandelier. Anarchy, ever my hero, took the cat off our hands, and I'd thought the problem solved. Foolish me.

"Well, I think it's exciting, getting a second chance at love. I hope the two of you are coming to the party on Saturday night."

I put thoughts of meatballs in grape jelly out of my head and forced a smile. "We wouldn't miss it."

CHAPTER THREE

*D*riving home with the top down, the wind had its
naughty way with my hair.

I parked the TR6 in the circle drive in front of the house,
smoothed the tangled strands that had pulled loose from my
ponytail, waved at Marian Dixon, whose binoculars glinted
behind her front window, and grabbed my handbag from the
passenger seat.

My front door opened, and Anarchy stepped outside and
grinned at me.

I stared. This man, with his movie star looks and eyes the
color of perfectly brewed coffee, was mine. My heart seemed
too large for my chest. Who cared about cold coffee? The
honeymoon was *not* over.

"Hey, you." He hurried down the steps, leaned forward, and
kissed me as I got out of the car.

Kissed me. Outside. Where the neighbors might see. I could
almost hear Marian's gasp as she pressed her binoculars closer
to her face. I didn't care.

"Hey," I whispered against his lips. "How was your day?"

"Better now." His lips grazed the shell of my ear. "Have we shocked the neighbors?"

"Definitely. Let's do it again."

He rewarded me with a chuckle. "Where have you been?"

"The pool."

He put a few unwanted inches between us and searched my expression as if I were easy to read. "Lots of people there?"

"A fair number."

"You heard." His voice was flat, as befitted murder.

"About Prudence's mother?"

He nodded.

"Suffocated with a pillow in her bed?"

His brows lifted. "How do you know that?"

"Jinx."

His eyes flashed with respect (or annoyance). "That woman knows everything. Peters is the lead detective."

"Is he?"

"He's coming over tonight. He has questions."

Peters had questions? For me? I had an airtight alibi. I'd been in Italy with my new husband. But my innocence never got in the way of Peters treating me like a suspect. My stomach tied itself in an intricate knot.

Anarchy's forehead creased as if he'd read every thought in my head. "He knows you didn't kill Mrs. Jarrett, but he has questions."

Maybe I was easy to read. "What about moving your things?"

"When we're done, he'll help shlep boxes."

"But why? What questions?"

"People talk to you. Those same people treat Peters like gum on the soles of their shoes. They tell him nothing."

My face tightened. "Why not ask Jinx?"

Anarchy smoothed a crease in my forehead with the brush of his finger. "We ought to put that woman on the payroll. But, we trust you."

While that was gratifying, having Peters join us at the house was not the romantic first evening home I'd envisioned. And tomorrow night promised even less romance. "I told Mother we'd have dinner with her and Daddy tomorrow night, but Grace has a swim meet. I need to call and let Mother know we can't come." She wouldn't be pleased.

"A swim meet? Am I invited?"

"You want to come? Imagine over-heated concrete crowded with kids and their parents, nerves, sweat, and gallons of gin."

He grinned. "Sounds fun."

"I'll make sure you're a timer." I wouldn't. No first-timer deserved that hellish job.

"Fine."

"Also, I accepted an invitation to a party on Saturday."

"At?"

"Sarah and August Elmhurst's."

"Have I met them?"

"They came to our reception. We'll have dinner with Libba and Charlie before we go. Libba wants Chinese."

"Okay." He smiled at the Dixon's house.

"What? Why are you smiling?"

"Can't you feel it?"

"What?"

"Your neighbor's stare."

"I'm too accustomed to it." I glanced over my shoulder at Marian's house. "She's definitely watching. She might be calling."

"Your mother?"

I nodded, then lifted onto my tiptoes and kissed him. "Calling to tell her about our scandalous behavior."

"I'll show her scandalous." He deepened the kiss, and I actually felt Marian's disapproval more relentless than the sun above us scald my skin.

Anarchy and I separated. Both breathless. And Anarchy tugged me toward the door. "Come inside, Mrs. Jones."

My stomach fluttered. "Is Grace home?"

"No."

My heart skipped a beat. "What about Aggie?"

"Running errands."

My pulse quickened. "Max?"

"Next door with Pansy."

Warm honey replaced the blood in my veins. "We have the house to ourselves?"

"Exactly. Let's not waste a minute."

A horn drew our attention, and we both turned.

"Damn," Anarchy muttered.

I simply stared. A disreputable pickup truck pulled into my —our—driveway. "Peters?"

"Yep."

"He has terrible timing."

"No argument." Anarchy's fingers tightened their grip on my hand, and together we waited on the stoop.

When Aggie first came to work for me, she drove a Beetle held together with duct tape, chicken wire, and love. Compared to Peter's truck, Aggie's Beetle was luxurious. "Is that thing road-worthy?"

"He got it here."

Whether he could make it go away was another question. My shoulders tightened as I anticipated the neighbors' complaints about the moldering hunk of metal now parked behind my shiny Triumph.

Peters climbed out of his truck and waved. "Welcome home."

"Thank you." I owed my ability to speak to rote manners. Inside, I was too shocked to form words. Peters never waved, never offered friendly words.

He reached into the truck's cab and pulled out a box. Not a box. A carrier. Whatever was inside yowled.

I groaned. No wonder Peters was in such a good mood. He was getting rid of the cat.

"What?" asked Anarchy. "What's wrong?"

"The cat."

"Give him a chance."

"Tell that to Max."

Anarchy stepped forward and accepted the carrier. "Thanks for taking care of him."

"No trouble," Peters replied.

I refrained from rolling my eyes. McCallester was nothing but trouble. "Please, come in."

I preferred not to answer Peters' questions while wearing a swimsuit and cover-up. "If you'll give me a few minutes, I'll change."

Peters's lips thinned as if my taking time to change inconvenienced him.

"Ten minutes tops," I lied. Then I raced upstairs, grabbed a lightning fast shower, ran a comb through my hair, faced the telephone, steeled my spine, picked up the receiver, and dialed.

"Hello." Mother's autocratic voice tightened my shoulders.

"It's me. I made a mistake."

"Oh?" She did not sound surprised.

"Grace has a swim meet tomorrow. We can't come for dinner."

Mother's answering silence was laden with disapproval.

"I apologize. I didn't remember the meet when we spoke this morning."

She tsked. "Come on Thursday."

"I'll check the calendar."

This time her silence was so heavy my shoulders bent beneath the weight.

"We'll be there on Thursday. May I bring anything?"

"Just be on time." Five-thirty for cocktails with dinner served at six-thirty.

"We'll be there. Goodbye." I hung up the phone and headed downstairs, where I found Anarchy and Peters seated at the kitchen island. A beer bottle sat in front of Anarchy while Peters sipped ice water. McCallester curled in Anarchy's lap.

I eyed the cat, and the dratted animal lifted a brow as if daring me to shove him off Anarchy's lap. I swallowed my annoyance. "Would you like anything stronger?"

Peters grimaced. "I can't."

"On duty?"

"So to speak. What can you tell me about Muriel Jarrett?"

"Hold on." I poured myself a glass of wine then settled next to Anarchy.

McCallester's eyes narrowed to slits, as if he were contemplating shredding my skin.

I ignored the threat. "You met her."

Peters rubbed his chin. "I did? When?"

"In the ladies' lounge at the country club. Bird thin. Horse teeth." She had that in common with her daughter. "An ebony cane with a handle shaped like a raven's head. She brandished it at you when she objected to your presence." The image of Muriel in her silk dress and sensible pumps brandishing her cane like a sword was burned in my brain.

"She didn't want me at the club?"

"She didn't want you in the ladies' lounge." Or the club.

"I don't remember her."

"Lucky you. She was a mean-spirited, self-important witch."

He snorted. "Tell us how you really feel."

"Prudence is awful, but she comes by it naturally."

He scratched at his mustache. "Is Mrs. Davies awful enough to kill her mother?"

"Yes. No." Honestly, I couldn't decide. "Maybe."

"Can you think of anyone else who hated Mrs. Jarrett enough to kill her?"

I'd avoided Muriel whenever possible and knew next to nothing about her. "Not off the top of my head."

"Because—" Peters raked a hand through his already messy hair "—the way she died was up close and personal."

I hoped, for Muriel's sake, she'd died in her sleep.

Anarchy looked up from stroking McCallester's striped back. "Prudence has an alibi, but we can't corroborate it. And it's possible someone snuck into the house."

"The missing key?"

Peters' face darkened and his brows drew into one bushy line. "How do you know about that?"

"Jinx."

He and Anarchy exchanged a loaded glance.

I swirled the wine in my glass. "What reason would Prudence have to kill her mother?" Aside from the obvious— they were both awful women.

"She'll inherit."

That was a reason. Muriel had been loaded. "Everything?"

"The bulk of the estate."

"Why now?"

Peters shook his head and stared at a cabinet. Anarchy picked at his beer bottle's label. Neither met my inquiring gaze. There was something they weren't telling me.

I sipped, then asked, "Where does Prudence say she was?"

"Meeting a friend who didn't show."

"At?"

"A jazz bar called Milton's. They were busy that night and no one remembers seeing her."

Milton's was always busy. "Prudence called me this morning."

Peters' mustache twitched. "What did she want?"

"I didn't speak to her." Anarchy and Peters were hiding something, and I wanted to know what it was. "What happened the night Muriel died?"

Peters tugged at his mustache. "Mrs. Jarrett went to bed around ten."

I put my glass on the counter and folded my hands in my lap. "You're certain of the time?"

"Mrs. Jarrett and her friend, Sally Billings, spoke on the phone. Mrs. Jarrett mentioned she was headed to bed. The two ladies spoke every night. Also, according to Mrs. Billings, Mrs. Jarrett said Mrs. Davies was out and at it again."

"What is 'it?'"

"She didn't specify."

I could guess. Prudence was sleeping (a euphemism if there ever was one) with a man she shouldn't.

"Mrs. Davies claims she arrived home at midnight."

"Do you have a time of death?"

"Between ten and twelve. The coroner leans toward earlier."

"Did Mrs. Jarrett usually go to bed at ten?"

"She made a habit of watching the ten o'clock news in bed."

It was a thirty-minute broadcast.

"According to Mrs. Davies, her mother's television was on when she arrived home. She tiptoed into the bedroom and turned it off."

"She didn't notice her mother was dead?"

"She believed her mother was sleeping."

"Who discovered Muriel?"

"The housekeeper. She brought her coffee at eight and found the body."

"When did you realize it was murder?"

"Immediately. There were purple splotches in her eyes, consistent with suffocation. Also—" Peters shot Anarchy a quick questioning glance.

My husband nodded.

"Also, we found a scrap of the pillowcase in her mouth."

"She tore it?"

He nodded.

"So she was awake?"

His lips thinned, and he gave a grim nod.

I reached for my wine. "How awful."

Neither man disagreed.

"So what do you want to know?"

"Did something happen between Mrs. Jarrett and Mrs. Davies that led to murder?"

How would I know? I'd been in Italy. "The inheritance?" I guessed. "Maybe Prudence needed the money."

Peters skewered me with a pointed stare. "This goes no further."

"What?"

"What I'm about to tell you."

"I promise."

"Mrs. Jarrett had cancer. If Mrs. Davies wanted the money, she had less than six months to wait." They weren't convinced of Prudence's guilt.

I let that settle. "What do you want from me?"

"I have questions."

"For whom?"

"Sally Billings."

Difficult, but not impossible. Sally's daughter Hazel had a son on the swim team. "What do you want to know?"

Peters tugged on his mustache. "Anyone who had a motive to kill Mrs. Jarrett."

"That's not easy to slip into conversation."

"I have faith in you," said Anarchy.

McCallester snickered. He had no faith. Not a bit.

I finished my wine. "I'll do my best."

～

Brown.

Anarchy lived in a sea—an ocean—of brown. Who knew one

little house could be so brown?

When an artist wanted brown, they mixed red and blue and yellow. There were shades—coffee (my personal favorite), hickory chocolate, umber, cedar, and pecan—but at the end of the day, brown was brown.

Brown shag.

Brown paneling.

Brown tweed upholstery on the couch facing a dark television screen that reflected brown.

Brown and harvest gold plaid curtains at the window.

Oh dear Lord. What did he want to take back to our house? Brown wasn't part of the décor palette.

He read my face. "The house came fully furnished."

This brown didn't belong to him. Thank God. My lungs reinflated.

"Not swanky enough for you?" A sneer tilted Peters's mustache.

"It's very monochromatic."

"You mean brown," said Anarchy.

"I do."

Anarchy's lips quirked.

"What are we packing?" The sooner we started, the sooner we could get out of this terrible rental.

"This way." He led us past a small brown kitchen (the linoleum on the floor looked like brown brick) to two closed doors. "Bedroom and study."

I readied myself for more brown.

Anarchy opened the bedroom door.

Brown shag carpet covered the floor. A brown quilted spread covered the bed. At least the walls were white. They were also covered with art.

I forgot the brown and stepped into the room. Thomas Hart Benton sketches, what looked like an Andrew Wyeth (mostly brown), and a painting of a golden wheat field beneath a stormy sky hung on the walls. "Is that a John Rogers Cox?"

"It is."

"I had no idea you were into regional art."

"I'm not. I just liked them." He led me to the second door. "There's more."

"More brown?"

"Yes," he admitted. "But also more art." He opened the door to an office. Brown carpet (no surprise). Brown drapes (the nubby kind that made my skin crawl).

My jaw dropped. "Is that a Carlo Mollino protractor desk?"

He nodded.

"With an Eames chair?"

Again, he nodded.

My gaze went to the walls. "A Hockney? Because you liked it?" My gaze traveled to the next painting. "Same with the Warhol?"

"Yep."

"How does a man who buys art like this—" I pointed at the Hockney "—live with all this brown?"

"I knew it was temporary."

"And this jacket?" I touched his plaid (tan and yellow and two shades of blue) covered arm. "You picked that Warhol and this jacket?"

His cheeks darkened.

A wave of remorse swamped me. Men weren't always good with clothes. "I apologize. I didn't mean to offend you. I'm just overcome by the art."

"You didn't offend me. I hate shopping for clothes."

So he walked into a store and bought the first thing he saw? That was a bad plan. "I dragged you to half the stores in Italy."

"Watching you shop is fun. It's like watching Leonard Bernstein conduct an orchestra, or John Wooden coach the Bruins."

I recognized Leonard Bernstein's name and assumed

Anarchy meant the comparison as a compliment. But what was a Bruin? I refused to be distracted. "Where did you get this jacket?"

"It was a gift."

"From?"

"My mother."

"Your mother shops for you?" I couldn't miss the tightness around his mouth or the sudden firmness of his jaw. Too late to keep the disbelief and judgment out of my voice. I tossed my hair over my shoulder and said, "She can retire. I'm taking over your wardrobe. As for this—" I waved at the desk and walls "—are we packing the small things?"

He blinked.

"Your vanity box, files, toiletries?"

"I thought we'd move it all."

I stared at him. Was he kidding?

He stared back, serious as a heart attack.

"We can move the chair," I ceded. "But the desk and the art need special treatment."

"I have quilts."

"We're not putting a Hockney in the bed of Peters's truck."

"What's wrong with my truck?"

"Not one thing." If one liked rust, rattles, and dubious suspension. "But the art should be boxed."

"Wow," said Anarchy.

"What?"

"You sound like Frances."

"Just what every bride wants to hear. She sounds like her mother." And in this case, Mother would be completely right. "The art is too good to risk damaging it in Peters' truck. I'm hiring a mover."

An expression I didn't recognize flashed across Anarchy's face.

"What?" I demanded.

He pretended innocence. "What do you mean?"

"You looked guilty."

"Me?" He inspected his fingernails.

"Definitely guilty. You drew your lips away from your teeth and winced."

He gave up studying his cuticles and rubbed a palm across his face. "My mother may ship a few things from California."

"A few things?" My voice was faint. "What kind of things?"

"Furniture. Now that I have a permanent address, she's done storing it."

"Okay." I drew the word out as my brain worked furiously. Our house was fully furnished. Where would we put Anarchy's furniture? And, while I was a fan of the desk, and it could happily live in Anarchy's study, mixing ultra-modern furniture with my antiques might be a disaster. And that was assuming his furniture was ultra-modern. What if he had a pair of plaid recliners? A set of bean bag chairs? We'd need a decorator. "Are we talking a chair? A table? A few lamps?"

He rubbed his palm, covering his mouth, and his words were muffled.

"What? I didn't understand."

"A truck."

"How big a truck?"

"No idea."

"Okay." Inside I screamed and stomped my feet. "When is the truck arriving?"

"Sometime this week. My mother was cagey about dates."

I stared at him. "This week?" And he was just now telling me?

"I didn't find out till this morning. Mom called the office and left a message."

"Where will we put it?" The house couldn't absorb much furniture.

"We'll get a storage unit." He wrapped an arm around my shoulders. "Don't worry, I'll handle the whole thing."

Men said that. And they meant it. And it never turned out well for the women in their lives. I had complete faith in Anarchy. Really, I did. So why did I feel as if something was about to go terribly wrong?

CHAPTER FOUR

I breezed into the card room at that club and stopped in my tracks. "You're early."

Daisy, who was never early, offered me a satisfied grin and stretched her shoulders. "The kids are at the pool with a sitter. I love summer."

In June, when the pool was a novelty, chlorinated water and summer friends and frozen Snickers bars kept children enthralled. By August, they'd be bored by the whole thing. "Are the kids on the swim team?" I asked. A silly question. Like me, Daisy wore the club colors. Obviously we'd both decided to arrive early, find a good parking spot, and keep it.

"Swim team gives us some structure."

I remembered those days. Children thrived on routine. Without the daily necessity of getting ready for school, they could easily turn into little sloths. And it didn't get better. Grace, a teenager, would sleep till noon without swim team and a job to get her out of bed. "How many swimmers do you have tonight?"

"Just two. The swim coach must hate me. Billy is swimming medley relay and Lilly swims free relay."

There were seven events in a swim meet. Medley relay was first. Free relay was last. It sounded easy enough, but there were six age groups divided by sex. That meant eighty-four races. "So you'll be staying for dinner?"

She groaned. "It's not as if I have time to cook, but the youngest is a bear by seven-thirty. Also, Billy and Lilly will be crushed if we skip the party." The post-meet party was the reward for enduring the meet. Mothers, exhausted by whining children and hours spent on concrete three degrees cooler than the surface of the sun, dove head-first into icy gin and tonics. Children, who'd already wheedled four or five treats from the snack bar, scarfed a kid-friendly buffet. Fathers, who arrived when the heat faded, rolled up their sleeves and doled out indulgent smiles. How hard could it be to corral volunteers, stage eighty-four races, and provide ribbons complete with the race, date, and child's time?

Hard. The logistics of a country club swim meet could befuddle a five-star general.

"Enough about swim." Daisy waggled her brows. "You're back from your honeymoon. Tell me everything."

I blushed.

Then Daisy blushed. Any woman with as many children as Daisy had no business blushing. "Not everything," she amended. "Just the G-rated parts."

"Italy was fabulous."

"Of course. It's Italy. Favorite meal?"

"A trattoria in Rome."

"Favorite purchase?"

"That's a tough one. Boots from a cobbler in Milan. They'll arrive in time for fall."

"Favorite art?"

"That's impossible." My mind still spun with the art we'd seen.

"Was it utterly romantic? I keep imagining you and Anarchy

in Rome, like Audrey Hepburn and Gregory Peck. Except you end up together. Did you ride a Vespa? Tell me you rode a Vespa."

"We rode a Vespa." While *Roman Holiday* made Vespa riding look cosmopolitan and romantic, the reality was quite different. Drivers in Rome were insane. I'd clutched Anarchy's midriff and gone rigid with terror. "It wasn't like the movie." I fanned the cards on the table.

"I should have asked. Is Grace swimming tonight?"

I nodded.

"Which events?"

"She didn't tell me. I'll find a heat sheet at the meet."

Daisy sighed. "How many more years do you have?" She made swim meets sound like time served in a gulag. She wasn't far from wrong.

"After this summer, two."

"Lucky. I'll be timing swim meets till I'm old and gray."

"Then stop having children." Jinx spoke from the entrance to the card room. "You do know how babies are made?"

"Very funny." Daisy, who spent too much time with people under the age of ten, made a horrible face, complete with puckered lips, wrinkled nose, and scrunched brows. "Shall we draw for deal?"

"What about Libba?" asked Jinx.

"I'll draw for her." I pulled two cards from the fanned deck. "This one's mine." I turned the jack of diamonds. "This is Libba's." I turned a nine of spades.

Jinx drew the queen of hearts, and Daisy pulled the two of clubs.

"Looks like I'm dealing," said Jinx. "Are these made?"

"I'm not sure." Daisy claimed the blue deck and shuffled.

Jinx shuffled the red deck a few times. "Ellison, will you cut?"

"Thin to win."

Jinx dealt the cards into neat stacks. "Did you ask Anarchy about Muriel Jarrett?"

"I did."

"And?"

Muriel Jarrett had cancer! "I have nothing new to tell you."

Jinx gave me a side-eyed scowl and snorted her disbelief.

"Am I late? I'm sorry." Libba slipped into the open chair across from me.

Jinx tapped the card table with a pink frosted nail. "Let's play."

I cast about for a topic other than Muriel Jarrett's murder. "Sarah Elmhurst told me about Sabra and the Tiki bartender. How on earth did Shirley and Dan keep that quiet?"

"I met him," said Daisy. "The Tiki bartender. His name is Jack."

That drew all eyes.

"Where did you meet?" Jinx demanded.

"The waiting room at the pediatrician's."

We gaped at her. Men didn't take children to the doctor. Men pointed at their son or daughter whose nose ran, ears ached, throat hurt, or skin itched and said, "Dick (or Jane) needs to see a doctor." Then they returned to their paper or the evening news and expected their wives to make it happen. Henry, who was fond of both the evening paper and Water Cronkite, never even knew Grace's doctor's name.

"He was at the pediatrician?" I confirmed.

Daisy nodded. "With Rainbow."

"Sabra named her baby Rainbow?" A girl named Rainbow didn't grow up to be a doctor or a lawyer or a banker. Mother-worthy disapproval tightened my face.

Jinx picked up her cards. "You talked to him?"

Daisy arranged her hand. "I did."

"And?" Jinx prompted. "What did you talk about?"

"Croup."

"That's all?" Jinx's face was a study in disappointment. Croup was hardly gossip.

"He said he was new to Kansas City, and I asked what brought him here."

"And he said?"

"Family."

"Where was Sabra?"

"Not at the doctor's office."

Jinx's eyes looked into the middle distance as if she were considering ramifications, then she tapped her lips with a manicured finger. "One club."

I had nine points. "Pass."

"One spade," Daisy responded.

Libba folded her hand. "Pass."

"Three spades," said Jinx.

I put my closed cards on the table. "Pass."

Daisy stared at her cards as if they held the secret to the universe. "Four spades."

Libba passed. So did Jinx. So did I.

Libba led the ace of diamonds, won the trick, and played the two.

I played the king, and Daisy played a trump from her hand then took the next eleven tricks.

"How many points did you have?" asked Jinx.

"Seventeen."

"Why didn't you ask for aces? You could have used Blackwood." The convention allowed Daisy to bid four no-trump, to which Jinx, who'd held a single ace, could answer five diamonds. Then Daisy, who'd held two kings, could have bid five no-trump. With her one king, Jinx's response was six diamonds. Daisy's final bid would be six spades. Which she'd made.

"It's the first hand, and you get—" Daisy's teeth sank into her lower lip, and she smoothed the ultra-suede cloth on the table.

"I get?"

"You get snippy if I go down the first hand." Daisy's words came in a rush.

"Snippy? I do not."

Libba snickered. "You do. Every time we play. You say there's only one way to go from here."

Jinx harrumphed. "Back to the Tiki bartender."

"His name is Jack," Daisy replied. "What about him?"

"What family?"

"I assumed Rainbow."

Jinx cut the cards. "You know what assuming does."

"Are you calling me an ass?" There was no heat in Daisy's words.

"Of course not." Jinx lit a cigarette and blew a plume of smoke into the air. "But you have a deplorable lack of curiosity. Be more like Ellison. Or me."

"Ellison is only curious when she finds a body," said Libba.

I gave Libba a tight, insincere smile. "You're so charming when you're sarcastic."

"That wasn't sarcasm."

After an afternoon in the air-conditioned clubhouse, the pool deck seemed especially hot. A bead of sweat (the first of many) trickled between my breasts. The overheated stew of swim meet season had me wiping my brow, and the sun beat on my shoulders as if it held a grudge against me.

Daisy waved a hand in front of her face in a futile attempt to move the humid air. "Lord, it's hot. Swim meets are like childbirth. Something in me deliberately erases the awful." She pulled a ponytail holder from her pocket and lifted the hair from her neck. "Are you volunteering tonight?" Each family was required to fill two volunteer slots per swim season.

"I have a double next week. You?"

She grimaced. "Tent monitor."

"Oh dear Lord." Riding herd on over-excited children hopped up on sugar and soda pop was even worse than timing races. "How?"

"Josie caught me at a weak moment."

"I'll bring you a cocktail at five."

"You're an angel. Wish me luck." She shuffled off to hell.

I stopped at the temporary bar and ordered an iced tea.

"Ellison, you're back." Josie Grimshaw was the volunteer chairman (a thankless job at which she excelled). She was unfailingly pleasant, unbelievably organized, and seldom had time for small talk at meets. If she'd stopped to speak with me, she wanted something.

I grew wary. "We got home a few days ago."

"I'm glad you're here. I don't suppose you'd—"

"I'm signed up for a double shift next week."

"Thank you for that. Meg Harrison hasn't arrived, and we need a timer."

"This is Anarchy's first swim meet. I planned on sitting with him." Not that we'd sit. We'd stand, chase patches of shade, and throw back iced tea until five o'clock when I would switch to gin and tonics.

"Of course. I understand. Let's chat later." She didn't have time to convince a newlywed to abandon her new husband. She needed a warm body to fill the shift.

Guilt poked at me. *Help her.* I ignored its sharp finger, sipped my tea, and stepped into shade cast by the clubhouse.

"Mom." Grace joined me out of the sun. She wore a new swimsuit, a racer-back with a blue background and strings of red bubbles.

I stared at the fabric. "Wow."

She struck a pose. "It's the new team suit. Awesome, right?"

Not the word I'd pick. "What are you swimming?"

"IM, free, breast, back, and free relay." She grinned. All teeth.

"Congratulations."

She glanced over her shoulder as if she expected eavesdroppers. "You may have a problem." Her voice was barely a whisper.

"Me?"

"I bumped Laine Jackson from the relay team."

To say Elaine Jackson's mother, Connie, was competitive was like saying Luciano Pavarotti was a middling tenor (I attended his debut solo recital at William Jewel and left certain of his greatness). "Thanks for the warning." I put avoiding Connie high on my to-do list.

Her smile wavered. "It's hard."

She felt bad about bumping her friend from a race? I offered an encouraging smile. "You earned that spot."

"Not that." She frowned at my obtuseness. "This is my first swim meet without Dad."

My late husband had invariably shown up as the shadows grew long, just in time for cocktails. With a martini in a plastic cup (no glass on the pool deck), he'd stand next to the water and shout himself hoarse, urging Grace to kick harder, swim faster, or focus on her form. He found her after each race and congratulated her, told her how proud he was. That didn't change. Ever. Didn't matter if the ribbon she received was blue or pink.

"He loved you."

She covered her mouth, blinked back tears, and nodded.

I gave her a moment.

"I'm happy for you and Anarchy, but I miss him."

"Of course you do." Henry had been a lousy husband and a good father. "You still have me and Aunt Sis and your grandparents and Anarchy."

"Thanks, Mom." She glanced toward a group of waiting girls. Girls who didn't have the sense to step out of the sun. "I should go."

"I'll be cheering."

"I know."

"I'm here if you need me."

"I know."

"Love you."

"I know. Love you, too."

She disappeared with her friends, and I watched her go.

"I haven't seen her in ages. She's growing up." Hazel Wallace had joined me in the shade.

"They do that."

She sighed. "When they're two, it seems as if you have all the time in the world. You blink, and they're sixteen, and you realize there's only two years till they leave for college.

I shivered in the heat. "I don't want to think about that."

"Me neither. How was your honeymoon?"

"Fabulous. How's your mother?"

She tilted her head as if my question puzzled her. "Fine."

"I heard she was the last person to talk to Muriel Jarrett."

"That."

That.

"Mom is beside herself about Muriel's murder. They were friends their whole lives. They went to kindergarten together. Grade school. High school. College. They were in the same sorority."

Which meant Sally Billings knew Muriel's secrets. "Does she think Prudence..." I let Hazel fill in the blank.

"She does not."

Interesting. "Then who?"

"Honestly, she has no idea."

"Muriel didn't have any skeletons in the closet?"

"None that might lead to murder. Not according to Mom."

So she did have skeletons. I arranged my face into an expression of polite curiosity and hoped Hazel might say more.

She remained annoyingly silent.

"What's Billings swimming this afternoon?"

"Free, breast, butterfly and the free relay."

"Butterfly?"

"He's one of those weird kids who likes it."

"If Grace had to swim butterfly, they'd hear her complaining in Colorado."

"I hear she's anchoring the free relay."

"She didn't tell me she was swimming last." Typically the final swimmer was responsible for making up lost time or maintaining a lead. For a teenager, swimming anchor was a big deal.

"Connie Jackson's not happy. She chewed out Thatcher." Thatcher was the head swim coach. As a teen, he'd swum for a rival club. Now, as a college junior, he made coaching a summer job. According to Grace, the teenage girls on the team had terrible crushes on him.

I shrugged. "Grace had a better time." Swim was supposed to be a meritocracy. Faster times meant more races and spots on the relay team. *Supposed to be.* Loud, angry, competitive mothers had been known to upend that apple cart.

A tow-headed child ran past us, and Hazel called, "Mike Elliot, slow down!"

The child glanced over his shoulder, dodged a mother holding a baby, and kept running.

Hazel sighed. "I swear the lifeguards are raising that child. Becky drops him off for morning practice and doesn't pick him up till five. He should have a sitter, someone to keep an eye out for him. It's the other mothers who get him to tennis practice and make sure he doesn't eat French fries and ice cream for lunch."

Most mothers, like Daisy, hired sitters to keep an eye on their children. A few, brave enough to risk censure from the pool moms, let their children roam free. I tsked my disapproval.

"I should check in. I'm a first shift runner." Runners took the time sheets from the lanes to the scoring table. It was one of the better jobs. Ribbons was the best—those volunteers were usually placed at a table in the shade. Some clubs even put the ribbons table inside. Like next week (the reason I'd claimed a double shift).

"Would your mother mind if I called her?"

"Mind? Of course not. She won't tell you Muriel's secrets."

"Not even if it will help catch the killer?"

"You can try." Her tone said I'd be wasting my time.

"Good luck to Billings."

"And to Grace." Hazel stepped into the sunshine, paused, and turned back to me. "Call Mom and say to her what you said to me. About catching Muriel's killer. She might talk to you."

"Thanks." I took a large sip of iced tea and surveyed the growing crowd. The visiting team warmed up in the pool while their mothers chatted and watched. The youngest members of our team were huddled in the shade of a temporary tent. Their mothers, sure that Daisy was riding herd, were elsewhere.

"Ellison." Connie Jackson had snuck up on me.

"Connie, how nice to see you."

"So, Grace is swimming the relay."

I suppressed a sigh. "Yes. The anchor."

"Laine has a better free time than Jane Lewis. She should be swimming in that relay."

"Sounds like a discussion you should have with the coaches." Poor Thatcher.

"Have you ever noticed that Jane is the only Lewis child with any athletic talent?"

"I have not."

"It makes me wonder."

"Wonder what?"

"Is she Brian's?"

I stared at her. She was willing to throw a sixteen-year-old girl's parentage into question for her daughter's spot on the free-relay team? "You're kidding."

"The boys are barely B swimmers."

"Connie, are you seriously suggesting Jane isn't Brian's? Because that's despicable."

She gasped as if I'd slapped her, then her expression hardened. "I bet there are at least five children on this pool deck who are calling the wrong man 'Dad.'"

"If you have a problem with Laine's races, take it up with the coach or the swim chair. Don't go after a child."

Her eyes narrowed. "Easy for you to say."

"It should be easy for you." I spotted Anarchy at the check-in desk and took a step toward him.

"Don't tell me you wouldn't take up for Grace."

Connie had lost her ever-lovin' mind. There was no way I'd take out my anger or disappointment on an innocent child. I couldn't get away from her fast enough, but I paused and looked into her eyes. "Not like that."

Her scowl burned a hole through my back as I walked away.

CHAPTER FIVE

*W*e paused on the front stoop of Mother and Daddy's house, and I asked Anarchy, "You ready?"

He offered me a smile that didn't reach his eyes. "Sure."

"You look great." He wore khaki pants, a white shirt, a navy blazer, and Italian loafers. Not even Mother would be able to find fault. With him. She'd tell me my linen shift was the wrong color or length or both. That, or she'd complain about the skinny straps of Grace's sundress. I steeled my spine and tightened my grip on the bag that held Mother and Daddy's gifts from Italy. "Ring the bell, Grace."

Grace jabbed the doorbell, and a moment later, my father, Harrington Walford, answered the door.

"Welcome." He ushered us into the house, led us to the living room, and headed for the bar table. "Anarchy, what'll you have?" Daddy's bar held five scotches (three blends and two single malts), rye, bourbon, four brands of gin, vodka, rum no one ever touched, an unopened bottle of Dubonnet, Kahlúa, red wine, tonic, club soda, an array of glassware, and a bowl of neatly sliced limes. "I make a great Manhattan."

"Whatever you're having, sir."

My father, who was fond of desert dry martinis, Tom Collins, and scotch, reached for the gin. "Ellison? Grace?"

"A gin and tonic, please. Where's Mother?"

"Running late." Daddy glanced at his watch and frowned. "She should be home by now. Grace?"

"A Tab with two limes, please."

I sank into a wingback chair and watched Daddy pour. "Light on the gin, please."

"Oh?"

"Late swim meet."

"Say no more." He served me a light gin and tonic and Grace a highball filled with Tab, then poured gin into two highballs and topped them with a lemonade mixture from a glass pitcher. "Tom Collins. My favorite summer drink." He offered a glass to Anarchy.

"Thank you, sir."

"Lose the 'sir.'"

"What should I call you?"

Daddy frowned, as if Anarchy had asked a trick question. "Harrington."

"Thank you, Harrington. Cheers."

Daddy lifted his glass. "Cheers."

I sipped my drink. "It's not like Mother to be late."

"No," Daddy agreed. "But she said she had a million errands, and if she bumped into a friend, she might have lost track of the time."

A phone rang somewhere in the house.

Daddy took a chair near mine. "Tell me about Italy."

"It was wonderful."

His eyes sparkled, and he grinned at my new husband. "Did Ellison drag you to every gallery and museum in the country?"

"Only half of them," Anarchy replied.

"Every cobbler in the country?"

"Not quite. One per city." Anarchy shot me an amused glance. "Except for Florence. There were two in Florence."

"Because they're both artists." I'd defend that decision come what may. Both men were artists. "If I'm not mistaken, you're wearing loafers from a cobbler in Florence."

Anarchy stretched out his legs and admired his shoes. "You're right. There's Da Vinci, Caravaggio, Titian, and Giuseppe Ghiberti, the second cobbler."

I wrinkled my nose at him.

The housekeeper appeared in the doorway. "Mr. Walford?"

Daddy turned in his chair. "Yes?"

"The phone, sir. There's been an accident."

He rose. "Frances?"

"There's a doctor on the line."

The color bled from Daddy's face. The glass slipped from my fingers and thudded onto the floor. Gin and tonic soaked the carpet. Thank God I wasn't drinking red wine. Mother would kill me if I stained her rug. My heart clenched, and I stood and followed Daddy to the nearest phone.

He listened, his expression grim. "We're on our way, Dick." He hung up the phone.

"What?" I demanded. "What happened? How is she?"

"Car accident. She's in surgery."

Anarchy had followed us, and he held up a set of keys. "I'll drive. Which hospital?"

Daddy told him, and we piled into the car. Daddy sat next to Anarchy, and Grace and I took the back seat. She reached for my hand and held it tightly. "Granna will be fine. She's a force of nature."

Daddy made a strangled sound, half-laugh and half-sob.

A similar noise rose in my throat, but I forced it down. My free hand fisted and dashed the tears prickling my eyes. "Daddy, what did Dick say?" I presumed Dick was his golfing buddy and also the head surgeon at the hospital.

"Car accident. Surgery. We should come immediately."

Anarchy caught my gaze in the rearview and I read the promise in his eyes. He'd make calls as soon as he had access to a phone. He'd find out what happened. My stomach clenched. If this was what Mother went through whenever I was hospitalized (an all too frequent occurrence), I owed her an apology.

Anarchy sped, his hands sure on the wheel, his gaze on the road. We reached the hospital in record time.

Daddy was out of the car before it came to a full stop.

"Go with him," Anarchy instructed. "I'll park."

Grace and I accompanied my father into the emergency room where he spoke with the nurse behind the desk.

He turned to me. "She's still in surgery."

"I'll have someone take you to the surgical waiting room," said the nurse.

I waved aside her offer. "We know the way."

"I'll wait for Anarchy." Grace offered.

"Thank you." I gave her a quick hug and walked with my father to the waiting room. We passed through bland corridors, breathed antiseptic air, and prayed.

An attendant offered us a kind smile as we entered. "Mr. Walford?"

"Is my wife all right?"

"I'll let the doctor know you're here."

Daddy sagged.

I read his tortured thoughts. If Mother were okay, the woman would have told us.

"Let's sit." I led him to a chair.

"I can't." He dragged a palm across his face and stared sightlessly at an oatmeal-colored wall.

"Can't sit?"

"Can't imagine life without your mother."

Another wave of unshed tears prickled. "It's Mother. She'll be fine. It will take more than a car accident to stop her." It would take more than a Sherman tank to stop Mother. I wrapped my arms around Daddy's torso and hugged him.

My cheek pressed against the weave of his linen blazer. I drew in his comforting scent—fine fabric and Ivory soap—deep into my lungs and blinked back fresh tears. He patted my back and drew a ragged breath.

The woman who'd welcomed us approached. "Doctor will be out shortly. May I get you anything?"

"No, thank you." I stepped away from Daddy and swiped my fingers beneath my eyes. Mother curled her lip at women with smeared mascara. I would not turn into a deranged raccoon as I waited for news. She'd never forgive me.

"Water, please," said Daddy.

Grace joined us. "Any news?"

"Not yet. Where's Anarchy?"

"I told him where we'd be. He stopped to make a call. He knows the way."

As a family, we spent too much time in this hospital—especially in the ER and surgical waiting room. We all knew the way.

Daddy, unable or unwilling to sit on one of the Naugahyde-covered chairs, paced from a vapid picture of a sunrise beach to the check-in desk. New lines etched his forehead and cut from his nose to the corners of his mouth. His broad shoulders buckled beneath the weight of worry.

Grace sat next to me. "Where's the doctor?"

"The attendant said he'll be here soon."

"It's so empty tonight," she observed. Evening meant no scheduled surgeries. And apparently Thursday was a slow day for emergency surgery. Only one other family waited, an older man and a woman around my age. He read the evening paper while she knitted.

She looked up from her yarn, caught me staring, and offered a sympathetic smile.

I tried to smile back at her, but my lips refused.

She nodded as if she understood and returned to her knitting.

"What's taking so long?" Daddy stood in front of me with his arms crossed over his chest.

"I'm sure Dick will be here soon." A lie. I wasn't sure of anything.

"What's keeping Anarchy?"

I wondered the same thing. "If the accident report hasn't been filed, they'll need to track down the officer on scene."

"Oh." Daddy resumed his pacing

Grace slouched in her chair. "This sucks."

"Grace!"

"What?" She rolled her eyes. "It totally sucks. You're married. Things are supposed to be calm and happy. Instead Granna's in surgery."

My getting married and Mother's car accident were unrelated, but I understood what Grace meant. We needed dull. We needed normalcy. We needed to feel settled. Instead, emotion and worry boiled and billowed around us like an angry cloud.

I rose from the chair.

"Where are you going?"

"I don't know, but I can't sit."

I joined Daddy in front of the beach print. He studied the shoreline as if the sand and water held the key to Mother's survival. "It's a terrible picture."

"Awful," I agreed.

"I wonder who chose it."

Probably a committee of women who'd worked hard not to offend or upset anyone. No footprints in the sand that might suggest death. No children playing lest a parent with a child in surgery worry his son or daughter might not see the beach again. Just a misty, pink-tinged, vaguely hopeful sunrise.

"Ellison."

I turned and searched Anarchy's face. His lips were thin and his eyes serious.

"The accident," said Daddy. "What happened?"

"Frances was rear-ended at an intersection."

That didn't sound so terrible.

"The impact pushed her into oncoming traffic."

I gasped. Visions of Mother's car being t-boned flashed through my head.

I reached for Daddy's arm.

He shook beneath my touch. "I believe I'll sit down now."

We barely made it to the nearest chair before he collapsed. "Two cars hit her?"

Anarchy's lips thinned to a mere line. "Three."

Oh dear Lord.

"Where?" Daddy asked.

"Sixty-third and Wornall." Anarchy raked a hand through his hair. "The car that rear-ended her left the scene."

"Witnesses?" I asked.

He nodded. "It was a Lincoln Continental Mark III. Pastel blue."

"So a woman," said Daddy.

"No one saw the driver, Harrington. Just the car."

"Men don't drive pastel blue cars," Daddy replied.

"Wait." I held up a hand. I needed a few seconds to think, to visualize. "They hit Mother hard enough to push her into an intersection, and then what? They backed up and drove away?"

Anarchy winced. "Yes."

"Isn't that illegal? Leaving the scene, I mean."

"Yes."

"Harrington." Dick Pruett, one of Daddy's oldest friends,

interrupted us. Like Daddy, he had a presence. Salt and pepper hair, a strong jaw, and an air of utter competence.

Daddy stood and grasped his friend's outstretched hand. "How is she?"

"Still in surgery. There were internal injuries, possible spinal damage, and her left arm and leg are broken."

Daddy paled. "Internal injuries?"

"We got them."

Daddy exhaled.

"Spinal damage?" The thought of Mother confined to a wheelchair was horrible.

"We'll have to wait and see."

"How much longer will she be in surgery?" Daddy asked.

"The orthopedic surgeon is in there now. It won't be much longer. After recovery, she'll go to the ICU."

"The prognosis?"

"I'm guardedly hopeful."

Hopeful was good. "Thank you, Dr. Pruett."

Dick—Dr. Pruett—clapped a hand on Daddy's shoulder. "Keep the faith. I'll let you know as soon as she's in recovery."

"Thanks." Daddy looked like he too had been hit by a Mark III. His skin sagged, his shoulders hunched, and his never-a-strand-out-of-place hair was mussed.

Dick returned to the operating room, and I wished the hospital had a bar. Daddy looked as if he needed a martini.

"You heard Dr Pruett." I strived for optimism. "He's hopeful."

Daddy nodded, but I wasn't sure he heard me.

Grace, who'd listened to Anarchy's description of the accident and Dr. Pruett's explanation of Mother's injuries, shook her head. "I don't understand."

"What do you mean?" I asked.

"Did someone hit Granna on purpose?"

Three adults regarded her with slack-jawed surprise.

"I mean they pushed her into a busy intersection, then left."

She looked at Anarchy for confirmation. When he nodded, she continued. "Who does that?"

"Someone without insurance or a valid license," Anarchy replied.

"In a Mark III?" Grace's tone reflected her disbelief.

"Someone did this to Frannie on purpose?" Daddy looked positively gray.

We all looked at Anarchy. A homicide detective should have the answer

"It's most likely an accident." He didn't sound entirely convinced.

I imagined my hands on a steering wheel, my foot on a gas pedal, and a red light visible through the windshield. My foot searched for an imaginary brake. I couldn't hit someone on purpose. Not in a million years. First, the awful sound of metal crashing into metal. My shoulders tightened just imagining it. Then, there was the real possibility I might hurt myself. "It would be crazy to drive into another car."

"If someone was mad enough, they might not care. Has Granna crossed anyone lately?" Grace directed her question to Daddy.

"Grace." The last thing Daddy needed was the suspicion that someone had tried to murder Mother. "That's enough."

"She's fine, Ellison." Daddy managed a weak smile. "But Anarchy is right. Someone without insurance or a license hit Frannie."

"So what happens now? With the Mark III, I mean."

"The department will notify local body shops. If anyone brings the car in for repair, we'll have questions." Anarchy rubbed the back of his neck. "You don't know anyone with a baby blue Mark III, do you?"

"Not that I can think of," I replied.

Grace nodded with vigor, as if Anarchy had finally stepped onto the right path. "Mrs. Jarrett."

"What?" I gaped at her. "How do you know?"

"She pulled into the drive when I was at her house."

"Why were you at her house?"

"You sent me to pick up Pansy's things."

So I had. "You're sure about the car?"

She gave a decisive nod. "Positive. She got out and yelled at me."

"Why?"

"Because she was mean. All I did was ring the doorbell, and she waved her cane at me."

That sounded about right.

"Muriel Jarrett is dead," said Daddy.

Anarchy and I had a whole conversation in one glance.

I can check the Jarrett's garage, but I don't want to leave you.

We'll be fine. But hurry back.

You're sure?

Positive. What if the car is damaged?

His face tightened. *Then I'll arrest Prudence.*

"Stop it," said Grace.

"Stop what?"

"You're doing that thing."

"Thing?"

"That silent conversation thing."

That thing.

"What did you decide?" asked Daddy. He and Mother had held silent conversations for more than forty years.

"Anarchy will swing by Muriel's and check the car."

Daddy nodded his grim approval.

Anarchy gave me a quick hug, pumped Daddy's hand, and left us.

"What if I'm right?" asked Grace.

"Then Prudence has some explaining to do."

"Would she do this on purpose?"

"Of course not."

"You don't sound convincing," Grace observed.

Because I wasn't convinced.

"Oh, no." Daddy dropped his head to his hands.

"Daddy?"

"We forgot to call your sister." He regarded me with pleading eyes. "Will you do it? Please?"

Because we needed more drama. "Of course." I collected my handbag, found the nearest payphone, and called Marjorie collect.

"Ellison Jones calling. Will you accept the charges?" The bored operator hadn't a clue how much I didn't want to make this call.

"Collect? Are you kidding?" My sister's annoyance flooded the phone line.

"I'm at the hospital." I rushed the words before Marjorie declined the call.

"Fine," she huffed. "I'll accept the charges. What's wrong now?" Marjorie was always so empathetic.

"Mother was in a car accident She's in surgery. Daddy asked me to call."

Silence traveled the line. Finally, Marjorie asked, "How bad?"

"Bad. Internal injuries. Possible spinal damage, and her left arm and leg are broken."

"Is she..."

"She's still in surgery. Dick Pruett is guardedly hopeful."

"Should I come?"

"If it were me, I'd come." There were no guarantees in life. Dr. Pruett might be hopeful, but worry and fear had wormed their way into my gut. Mother might die.

"I'll have to rearrange my schedule." Marjorie sounded put out by the hassle of rescheduling her tennis lesson or massage or bridge game.

My free hand clenched into a fist. "If it's too much trouble, don't come." My life would be easier if Marjorie stayed in Ohio.

My sister had a way of sucking all the oxygen from a room. Also, she had a habit of making any situation about her. But Mother would be wounded if her oldest daughter didn't come. And Mother had sustained enough pain. Also, if the worst happened, and Mother—a chill iced my spine—no, I wouldn't go there. "I take that back. Get on a plane. Now."

"Fine. I'll leave in the morning."

I hoped she didn't arrive too late.

CHAPTER SIX

*G*race sat next to me in an uncomfortable waiting room chair and picked at her nail polish.

I refrained from comment.

Daddy paced.

"I can hear you," Grace muttered.

"I didn't say anything."

"You didn't have to. Picking at the polish is bad for my nails."

"I didn't say a word."

"If Granna—when Granna—wakes up and sees my hands, she'll have a coronary. Ladies don't go around with chipped nails." She mimicked Mother perfectly.

"My lips are sealed."

"Why?"

Because the me in her head was doing a better job scolding than the actual me ever could. "Because if picking your nail polish brings you a modicum of comfort, I won't say a word against it."

She creased her brow and tilted her chin toward the ceiling. "You can be really annoying."

"You mean arguing with me about your nails would be a better distraction than destroying them?"

"Yes," she huffed.

"Sorry to disappoint."

"I don't think you are."

"I think we have enough drama without a fight about your nails."

She huffed again.

The attendant, who was a few years older than God, offered me a sympathetic smile. What a terrible job she had, to watch families scored by worry and grief.

I stood.

"Where are you going?" asked Grace.

"Nowhere. I just need to move." Like father like daughter.

"She'll be okay, Mom."

The alternative was too bleak to consider

"Harrington." Dick Pruett appeared at the double doors to the operating rooms. "You can see her now." He offered Grace and me an encouraging half-smile. "She made it through surgery with flying colors. Frances is a fighter."

I offered a grateful nod, and Daddy followed Dick to the recovery room.

"What now?" asked Grace.

"I need to call Aggie." She'd want to know about Marjorie's arrival.

"She's not home. When we made dinner plans, she went out with Mac."

"Drat."

"What?"

"Marjorie will want the blue room The sheets need airing and we need fresh towels, and—"

"Aunt Marjorie is staying with us?" Grace sounded appropriately horrified.

"Daddy can't take her, and I can't send her to a hotel. Not in a crisis."

My daughter slouched in her chair. "Fine. I'll get the guest room ready."

"Aggie can—"

"Aggie won't come home tonight."

I blinked.

"She and Mac are serious, and she spent every night with me for the entire time you and Anarchy were in Italy. When Anarchy gets back from checking the Jarett's garage, he can run me home. I'll take care of the sheets and towels."

"You're a great kid."

"You mean when I'm not picking fights about nail polish? Sit." She patted the chair next to hers. "Please. All this pacing makes me nervous."

I sat and studied my hands in my lap. I couldn't throw too many stones at Grace's nails. I needed a manicure.

"I heard you and Mrs. Jackson got in a fight last night."

I looked up and shifted my gaze to Grace. "How'd you hear that?"

She rolled her eyes.

Right. In the summer, gossip spread across pool decks faster than Secretariat ran the Belmont Stakes.

"I feel bad for Laine. She doesn't care which races she swims or if she's A or B, but her mother..." Grace shuddered.

"It can be tough living up to a mother's expectations."

"Tell me about it."

"Very funny."

"Mrs. Jackson would have come after you even if Laine hadn't been bumped from the relay."

"Oh?"

"She didn't get into the garden club."

"How is that my fault?" I'd been at a café making moon-eyes at Anarchy when the membership voted on its new members.

Granna opposed her membership."

"Ah." Connie's beef was with Mother, not me. But no one wanted a fight with Mother. "I wonder why Mother opposed her?"

"You'll have to ask her." Grace took my hand and squeezed, then she straightened in her chair. "Did you find it?"

I followed her gaze.

Anarchy had returned.

I stood and went to him.

His arms wrapped me in a warm hug. "How's your mother?"

"Out of surgery."

"And?"

"Daddy's with her now. Dr. Pruett said it went well."

"Did you find the car?" Grace demanded.

"Prudence reported it stolen."

That was convenient. "When?"

"She says she noticed the car was gone when she arrived home at six o'clock."

Grace huffed her disbelief.

Even I, who couldn't imagine a reason Prudence would ram her mother's car into Mother, found the story too convenient. Why would she do such a thing? "Prudence has a license and insurance. If she was in a car accident, she wouldn't leave."

Daddy entered the waiting room and spotted Anarchy. "The car?"

"Stolen."

Daddy's lips thinned. Apparently he found that as suspicious as Grace and I did.

"It explains why the driver didn't stop," said Anarchy.

"Where was the car stolen?" Grace demanded. "The Plaza? Brookside?"

"From the garage."

Grace planted her hands on her hips and pursed her lips. "I don't believe it."

Daddy ran a hand across his tired eyes as if talk about the stolen Mark III pained him. "Ellison, they're taking Frances to the ICU. We can stay with her."

I turned to my husband. "Anarchy, will you take Grace home?"

"Of course."

Grace opened her mouth to argue, but I stopped her with a look.

"Fine." The word was grudging. "I'll take care of the sheets and towels. Anything else?"

Probably. But I couldn't think of it. "No."

"You'll call me if there's any change?"

"I promise."

She gave a grudging nod.

Anarchy kissed my cheek. "I'll be back."

"There's no telling how late we'll be, and you have work in the morning."

"Doesn't matter."

I didn't argue. I wanted him with me.

Daddy tugged on my arm. "We'll be in the ICU waiting room."

We walked into the hallway together, but Anarchy and Grace turned left while Daddy and I turned right. Together, we headed for the next waiting room.

My father's face was drawn and gray, and I cast about for something to distract him. "Grace told me Mother shot down Connie Jackson's membership in the garden club."

He frowned. "You think Connie Jackson did this? She's responsible?"

"Good heavens, no. I was making conversation." Although, it was easy to imagine Connie Jackson ramming someone's car if she thought it might benefit Laine. "Can you think of anyone who might—"

"No."

I patted his arm. "Okay."

"It's an accident. Has to be." He didn't say our family had met its murder quota with my first husband's death. He didn't say it, but the words hung above our heads like a ponderous cloud.

I chose a chair in the new waiting room and stared at a picture of a boat floating on a calm sea.

"You can see her after they get her settled."

"Okay." I clasped my hands in my lap and said a silent prayer. Long minutes passed, and I shifted in the uncomfortable chair.

"Mrs. Jones? "A nurse nodded at me.

"Yes." I stood.

"You can see your mother. Ten minutes."

"Is she conscious?"

"No. But she'll know you're with her if you hold her hand."

"Go, sugar," Daddy directed. "I'll be fine."

He looked the opposite of fine, but I followed the nurse into a private room, stopping when I saw Mother. Her face was a dark bruise. Her left arm and leg were in casts. An IV needle pierced her left wrist.

"You've looked better." The words just slipped out. Unbidden. If I was blurting things like that, it was a good thing she was unconscious. "You're going to be fine. You can spend the whole summer bossing me and Daddy."

Mother's right hand twitched.

"Anarchy and Grace, too."

That got me a second twitch.

"You can hear me?"

Mother gave a tiny nod.

"You were in a car accident, and you're in the hospital, but Dr. Pruett says you'll be fine. Daddy's in the waiting room. Do you want me to get him?"

Her answering nod looked as if it hurt her.

I hurried to the door and called, "Daddy!"

He came running.

"She's awake."

"Frannie." Daddy sank onto the chair to the right of Mother's bed and took her hand in his. "You scared me, Frances. I need you."

I watched them. Daddy, bent with his lips pressed to the back of mother's hand. Mother, beaten, but unbroken. The tension around my heart eased, and I tiptoed out of the room.

Anarchy and I stumbled (I stumbled, Anarchy held my arm) into the kitchen through the backdoor.

"Tired?" he asked.

Tired? Given the chance, I'd sleep for a week. A month. My stomach growled loud enough to earn an answering growl from Max. Or maybe he was growling at McCallester who sat in the center of the kitchen island, safe from the reach of Max's paws. The cat gazed at Max with enormous eyes as his tail swished from side to side.

Anarchy's forehead creased. "You missed dinner."

"So did you."

"I grabbed a sandwich when I brought Grace home. I'll fix you something." He led me to a stool. "Sit."

"It's too late to eat." The clock read ten minutes past midnight. Also, sleep.

He frowned. "You're sure?"

"Positive." My stomach growled louder than a muscle car.

"You should eat something." Anarchy opened the refrigerator and peered inside. "How about cheese and crackers?"

I was too tired to explain that I never ate within three hours of bedtime. And I was really hoping bedtime was less than fifteen minutes away. "Fine." A cracker with a bit of cheddar or

Gruyere wouldn't kill me. "But I need to do something first." I took a step toward the family room.

"What are you doing?"

"Answering machine. Marjorie may have left her flight information."

Max, who often followed me around the house, eyed Anarchy and the block of cheese in his hand, and let me go to the family room alone.

I switched on a lamp and crossed to my desk. The light on the answering machine blinked madly, and I pushed the play button.

It's Aggie calling. Mac took me to a new restaurant in Liberty, and his truck broke down. We're spending the night, and I won't be home till a mechanic can fix the doohickey. I'm sorry for any inconvenience. Hope your dinner went well.

Marjorie was coming, and Aggie was stuck in Liberty. I closed my eyes and sighed.

The light still blinked. Again, I pressed the button.

Ellison, it's your sister. My plane lands at seven. No need to pick me up. I'll take a cab to your house, drop my bag, and we can go to the hospital together.

Marjorie making things easy? It was official, hell had frozen over.

The light still blinked, and I jabbed at the button.

Ellison, Lloyd Foster on the line. I have a layover in Kansas City tomorrow and want to visit your studio. May I stop by around noon? His posh British accent made the most mundane question sound important. But this question wasn't mundane. *I'll call tomorrow and confirm.*

My shoulders sagged. When Lloyd called, I'd have to tell him not to come.

"Your snack is ready." Anarchy stood in the doorway holding a plate.

Max peered around his legs. My dog wore an if-you're-not-going-to-eat-that-I'll-be-happy-to-take-it-off-your-hands expression.

"You poor starving dog," I murmured. "You can't have cheese. It gives you gas." The kind that made the house unlivable for days.

"What's wrong?" asked Anarchy.

"Aggie's stuck in Liberty. Marjorie is staying with us."

"Why is Aggie stuck?"

"Mac's truck broke down."

"How bad?"

"A doohickey."

He grinned. "Technical term?"

"The one Aggie used. Also, Lloyd Foster called. He wants to see my studio tomorrow—today—at noon."

"Lloyd is coming?"

"He can't. There's too much—"

"He lives in London. When will you get another chance to show him your studio?"

He made a good point, but taking time for a gallery owner was impossible. "There's Mother. And Marjorie. And—"

"I'll take the day off work."

That stopped me. "Won't your boss object?" Anarchy was back two days from a two-week vacation.

"There are a few files on my desk. I'll take care of them first thing, then I can help you." He handed me the plate piled high with carefully cut cheese on round crackers. He'd even added a sprig of grapes. "Your mother is in the hospital. You need me."

More than I could say. My jaw ached with the effort not to cry, but a tear made it past my defenses.

"Hey, now." He wiped the wetness from my cheek. "No tears over cheese and crackers."

Cheese and crackers didn't make me cry. It was the thought behind them. And gratitude. It felt so wonderful to have someone who took care of me. Henry would no more have taken a day off work to help me deal with my family and job than he would have flown to the moon on one wing. "I'm a very lucky woman."

He took the plate from my hands, put it on the desk, and gathered me into his arms. "I'm the lucky one."

It was cute he thought that.

He frowned. "You're not done."

"What?"

"The answering machine. It's still blinking." He pressed the play button.

Ellison, it's Prudence Davis. We need to talk.

I stared at the answering machine as if it had just grown a second head (or a first one).

"Max! No!" Anarchy's warning came too late. With one sweep of his paw, Max knocked the plate of cheese and crackers to the floor. He hoovered up the cheese in less time than it took me to bend and fumble for his collar.

"Darn it, Max! Bad dog."

He ignored me and ate the crackers, chomping and dropping crumbs to the floor as if making a huge mess was his actual job.

The crumbs were the least of my worries. I pressed my palms to my forehead. "He ate cheese."

"Is that a bad thing?"

"I wasn't kidding about the gas." As a Weimaraner, Max carried a regal air. His coat shone like polished pewter. His eyes gleamed with rare intelligence. His head and body were ideal to the breed. Smoke and mirrors. My gorgeous, brilliant dog produces the worst odors on the planet. Bar none.

Anarchy laughed. "He's just a dog."

Within a few hours, Anarchy would learn not to laugh about Max and cheese. "You say that now. Just wait." Max was capable of creating a noxious cloud. One with surprising staying power. I could hear Marjorie's complaints already.

"That bad?"

"Just wait." I glanced at the answering machine. "I wonder what Prudence wants?"

"Only one way to find out." He meant call her.

Oh, joy. I had that to look forward to.

He took my hand and pulled me toward the kitchen. "C'mon. I'll fix you another plate."

"If it's okay, I'd just as soon go to bed."

Interest flared in his brown eyes. "As you wish, Mrs. Jones."

CHAPTER SEVEN

Brnng, brnng.

I pulled a pillow over my head. Someone had replaced my brains with wool, and I needed more sleep to be smarter than a sheep.

Brnng, brnng.

The pillow wasn't working, I still heard the phone. Whatever the time, it was too early for phone calls. Too early for more problems.

"Hello." Anarchy's voice was bright, as if he'd enjoyed a full night's sleep, not the seemed-like-five-minutes we'd managed.

I lifted the pillow, slitted an eye against the lavender light sneaking through the windows, and peeked at the clock. Six? Really? My face settled into a scowl. Who called at six?

Anarchy sat up. "I'll tell her." Worry tinged his words with a dark pall.

I went from that half-asleep to half-panicked in less than a second. "Is that the hospital? Is Mother all right?" When we'd left her, the doctors seemed optimistic.

He hung up the phone and nodded. "She's stable, but they want you to come right away."

I levitated out of bed.

Anarchy threw back the covers on his side. "I'll take you."

"What did they say?"

"Not much."

"But she's stable?" Stable was good. Or maybe stable meant there was just enough time to get to the hospital to say goodbye.

I ran a comb through my hair, washed my face, brushed my teeth, threw on a shift dress, and jammed my feet into sandals. Then I raced downstairs.

When I reached the kitchen, Anarchy handed me coffee.

My fingers tightened around the mug, and I drank gratefully. "They didn't say what's wrong?"

He shook his head. "Just that you should come as soon as possible."

He'd donned khaki pants and a crisp white dress shirt. His handsome face was lined with concern. Concern for me. Concern for Mother.

I tilted my head and gulped coffee like a college kid playing a drinking game, then put the empty cup on the counter. "Let's go." I paused and pinched the bridge of my nose.

"What?"

"I need to leave a note for Marjorie." Fortunately, my sister had a key to the house. She'd be able to let herself in.

"A note?"

"In case we're not here when she arrives."

"Grace—"

"Grace has swim practice, then she babysits. She may not be here."

"But—"

"Let's see how Mother is before we scare Grace. If it's bad, I'll call her. Otherwise, I'm going to let her be a kid." I hurried to my desk, pulled a piece of monogrammed stationery from a drawer, and jotted a few lines.

Marjorie, sorry I'm not here to welcome you. I was called to the hospital. Please meet me there. Ellison.

I left the note on the kitchen counter, filled a Styrofoam cup with coffee, and gave Max a quick scratch behind the ears. "Don't tear down the house and do be nice to your aunt."

He made no promises. Instead he passed gas, a sound like raspberries on a baby's round tummy. But louder. Twenty times louder. Max looked over his shoulder as if he wondered what created the noise.

I held a hand over my nose and gagged.

With a silent apology to Mr. Coffee (who couldn't escape), I stepped outside where the birds sang, a soft breeze rustled the leaves, and the scent of flowers perfumed the air. So much better than inside where Max's struggles with digesting cheese were thick as pea soup and ten times as smelly. "We should put him in the backyard."

Anarchy, who'd followed me, nodded. His skin was looking exceedingly green, and he kept a hand clapped over the lower half of his face. He opened the back door and called (through his fingers), "Max!"

Our dog trotted outside. He wore a pleased expression, and I wondered if he knew that he'd cleared the downstairs.

"I told you. Cheese and Max are a lethal combination."

"Lesson learned."

Easier to focus on the dog's gas than the absolute terror constricting my chest. Anarchy led me to the car, opened the passenger door, and I slipped inside.

We sped toward the hospital. At twenty after six, there were few cars to slow us down.

I took a sip of coffee. "I hate Styrofoam."

His brows lifted. "Pardon me?"

"Styrofoam. I don't like the way it feels on my lips." Thinking about the unpleasant plastic sensation was a good distraction.

"She'll be okay." Anarchy read me so easily. Were fear and sadness written across my face?

"What if she's not?" A world without Mother? The coffee in my stomach soured. Mother might be a bully and a snob and she could provoke a saint (and I was no saint). But she was also honest and loyal and she loved her family with singular focus. A sob caught in my throat. "What exactly did they say?"

"The nurse said she'd asked for you and that we should hurry."

Iron bands constricted my chest, and I struggled to draw air into my lungs.

Anarchy reached for my free hand. His fingers were warm and strong, and tears sneaked past my eyelids.

Rather than dropping me at the entrance, he drove us into the parking garage. "We'll go inside together." He didn't want me to face whatever waited alone.

Love and terror swelled my heart to the point of bursting. I gave his hand a grateful squeeze and nodded.

He parked and helped me from the car. I swayed slightly, and he wrapped an arm around my waist. "We're in this together."

I couldn't speak, so I nodded.

We entered the hospital, and the heels of my sandals clacked against the tile floor. "It's so empty," I whispered.

His hand on my waist tightened. His fingers were anchors, all that kept me from being swept into a sea of panic. "Visiting hours aren't for a few more hours." His voice was calm and comforting, but a sob rose from deep in my soul, and I pressed a hand to my mouth.

Anarchy stopped and gathered me into his arms. "No matter what, I'm here for you."

I rested my head against his chest. The feel of his hand rubbing small circles on my back kept me from drowning in a bottomless pool of sadness.

I took a deep, ragged breath. "I'm fine." Liar, liar. "Let's go." If

Mother had minutes left, I wanted to spend them with her, not crying in the hallway.

We approached the nurses' station, and Anarchy said, "We're here to see Frances Walford."

The nurse, a no-nonsense woman with gray eyes and blonde hair pulled into a tight bun, stared at me for long seconds. "You're her daughter."

"Yes." My voice was high and thin, as if my lungs no longer processed air. I couldn't bear the pitying expression on her face, so I looked at my feet. They were already tan, and the nails were painted a delicate pink. "Is she okay?"

"She's down the hall in—"

"We know the room number," said Anarchy. Together, we hurried toward Mother's room, slowing to take in the nurse standing in the hallway. Her face was bone white, and her hands shook like the fringe on Charo's costumes (but with less cutchi-cutchi, and more I-need-hoochy-hoochy).

"Are you her daughter?" she asked. "Are you Ellison?"

"Yes."

Her eyes filled with pity.

Mother was dying. I pressed my free hand to my stomach as my morning coffee threatened a reappearance. "Is my father here?"

"She asked for you." The nurse ran an open palm down her face. "I'm so sorry. You can go in."

With my heart hammering in my chest, I pushed open the door and stepped inside Mother's hospital room.

"What took you so long?"

The woman in the hospital bed was bruised, battered, blood-ied. And obviously not at death's door. "Mother? You're all right?"

"Answer my question."

"It's six-thirty. In the morning." In case she'd missed the time.

"Your point?"

"We were asleep."

She sniffed. "I had the nurse bring a pen and paper. Take notes."

"Wait." I needed a minute to process. I rubbed a hand across my face. "Why did you call for me?"

"I have a list and I can't write."

"I thought you were dying."

"From a car accident? Not likely." She frowned at my husband. "You brought Anarchy?"

"We got a call at six in the morning to come to the hospital right away. We thought the worst."

She sniffed. "First, call my bridge group. Let them know I can't make it today."

I gaped at her. "You got me out of bed at six, scared me nearly half-to-death, to call your bridge group?"

"So dramatic."

She'd dismissed my fears as dramatic? I'd show her dramatic. I clenched my hands into fists. "Mother."

She sighed as if I were inconveniencing her. "What, Ellison?"

"This is not okay. Have you never heard of the boy who cried wolf?"

We stared at each other, but it was hard to stare down a woman whose face was purple and black and swollen. One whose arm and leg were encased in plaster. One whose bottom lip quivered with unshed tears. Mother didn't want to be alone. Not that she'd admit that.

"Anarchy." I patted my husband's arm. "Would you see if the coffee shop is open? I desperately need coffee." I had things to say to my mother. Things she wouldn't forgive Anarchy for hearing.

He gave Mother a look that would terrify a lesser woman. "Sure."

When he left us, I perched on the edge of the chair next to her bed. "How could you?"

She wouldn't meet my gaze.

Mother always met my gaze. Met my gaze and scowled me into submission. Something was wrong.

"I woke and didn't know where I was. They said your father went home."

"He was here most of the night. He wanted a shower and a few hours' rest."

"I was alone."

I swallowed a sigh and picked up the pad of paper. "What else besides your bridge group?"

"I have a garden club committee meeting. You'll need to organize keeping your father fed. My friends will want to help, but you need to create a calendar. Also, we're supposed to have dinner with the Davidsons tonight. Call Shirley."

"None of this could wait till nine?"

Emotion flashed in her eyes, and for a second, it read as fear. It was as I suspected. Mother was afraid. She averted her gaze as if she realized she'd revealed too much. "Poor Shirley, this situation with Sabra has worn on her."

"The baby or the marriage or the father showing up?"

"Everything." Mother tsked. "That girl. Her older sibling never pulled anything like this." Twelve years separated Sabra from her brother, and fourteen from her sister.

"Maybe Shirley should have done a better job parenting." She'd handed her baby to her teenage daughter and returned to her bridge game.

"Sabra was an unwelcome surprise. Shirley was three-quarters of the way through the race, then she found herself back at the starting line."

"Not Sabra's fault."

"No," Mother ceded. "But she's responsible for her choices now."

"Daisy met the husband. She said he was nice."

The door opened, and Anarchy put a cup in my hands then glared at Mother. "You caused Ellison needless heartache."

Mother and I gaped at my husband who stood next to me, turning a coffee cup in his hands.

The silence was so heavy my shoulders sagged.

"You bullied the nurses into calling her," he continued.

Mother's eyes narrowed.

Anarchy's did too.

It was as if they'd both been possessed by Harry Callahan and were ready to reach for .44 Magnums.

"It was cruel."

Mother's mouth opened then closed.

My heart fluttered. I wasn't accustomed to anyone stepping into the breach for me. I sipped my coffee.

"Now, before you completely hijack my wife's day, did you see who hit you?"

Mother stared. So long, I thought she might not answer, but then she shook her head.

"It was a pale blue Mark III," he prompted.

"I don't remember the accident."

"Can you think of anyone who might want to hurt you?"

"You're suggesting this was deliberate?" Mother used her you've-lost-your-mind tone.

"It's a possibility." Anarchy's tone was suspiciously dry. As if he'd compiled a long list of reasons to kill Mother.

"That's ridiculous," she snapped.

"No." Anarchy put his coffee on the window ledge and crossed his arms over his chest. "It's not."

Again with the Harry Callahan impersonations.

I cleared my throat. "You blocked Connie Jackson's membership in the garden club."

My husband and my mother shifted their narrowed gazes my way.

"No one attempts murder over the garden club. Besides, it wasn't personal," said Mother. "There were seven candidates and only three spots available."

"She's a legacy," I replied. Legacies were usually shoe-ins.

"And she'll get in. Eventually."

"Are the new members legacies?"

Mother gazed at the ceiling as if the secrets of the universe were written on its surface.

"I'll take that as a 'no.'"

"Two were." The way she avoided my gaze made me certain her candidate was the non-legacy.

"Who did you get in?"

"Hazel Wallace."

"Why?"

"Sally asked me." Sally, who was not a gardener but was Muriel Jarrett's best friend.

"Since when do you do favors for Sally Billings?"

Mother's gaze flitted to Anarchy before landing on me. "Since your father is in negotiations with her husband's company."

"I see."

"This conversation is moot. Connie Jackson doesn't have the gumption to ram my car into an intersection."

"Someone does."

"It was an accident." Mother spoke with certainty born of denial.

Anarchy's expression was flat. "I'm not so sure about that."

"Shouldn't you be investigating actual murders?" Mother's tone could freeze the Missouri River. Solid. In the middle of summer.

"I am. Doesn't stop me from looking into an attempted murder."

They regarded each other—scowled at each other. The tension in the room was palpable.

Mother shifted. Winced. "Ellison, this pillow is unacceptable. You'll need to bring me pillows. Add them to the list."

She was deflecting.

Anarchy reached for his belt and scowled at his pager. "Frances." He nodded at the phone. "May I?"

"Of course."

He dialed. "Jones." The voice on the other end of the line was low, and Anarchy listened in silence.

Mother closed her eyes as if my husband's presence pained her.

I waited.

"Got it." Anarchy hung up the phone and turned his gaze on me. "A word?" He nodded toward the hallway.

"Of course."

We left Mother and walked toward the nurse's station.

"Your mother is manipulative."

"You don't say." I softened my sarcasm with a smile. "Nothing I can't handle. Right now, I'm grateful she's not dying."

"I have to go to the station. Are you okay here for a few hours?"

"Fine." I'd work my way through Mother's list.

"Peters will pick me up." He handed me the car keys. "I don't want you stuck here without a means to leave."

"Thank you."

"You're okay?"

"She's not dying. And Daddy and Marjorie will be along soon."

He leaned forward and kissed my cheek. "You're too forgiving. I love that about you."

I watched him walk to the elevator, then returned to Mother's room.

Three hours later, I returned the receiver to its cradle and glanced at my watch. I'd made two million phone calls, delegated the feeding of my father to Mother's housekeeper, and begun a list of my own. The floral deliveries had begun. Thus far, a potted orchid, a bouquet of Gerber daisies, and a Boston fern brightened the over-cooked-oatmeal shade of Mother's room.

"You'll have to write the thank-you notes," said Mother. "Or perhaps Marjorie can do that. She has better penmanship."

"I wonder where Marjorie is." I pictured her stretched on a chaise on my back patio, avoiding Mother's endless tasks. I picked up the receiver, called my home number, and drummed my fingers on the chair's arm as the phone rang.

"Jones' residence."

"Marjorie?"

"Ellison? I can't believe you did this to me."

"I am sorry. I got an emergency call at six. I thought you'd call a cab. I left a note."

"What are you talking about?"

"Leaving for the hospital before you arrived. What are you talking about?"

"The movers."

I got a sudden sinking feeling. "What movers?"

"The ones unloading furniture into your front hall. Also, what's wrong with Max? He smells like a garbage dump."

"He ate cheese. Movers?"

"From California. When did you get a cat?"

"How much furniture?"

"The study is full. And the dining room. They're filling the living room now."

Oh dear Lord.

She sniffed. "Did someone buy out a high-end antique store? Hold on. Put the rug in the family room."

"The rug?"

"Looks like a Tabriz. Palace size."

I dropped my head to my hands. "How much more?"

"The truck is big."

"How big?"

"A large truck, Ellison. A semi."

Sweet nine-pound baby Jesus, a semi?

"I take it this is a surprise."

To put it mildly. "Yes."

My sister, who fully embraced schadenfreude when it came to me, laughed.

CHAPTER EIGHT

I pushed open the front door, and the air left my lungs in one gigantic whoosh. My home resembled a warehouse. A packed warehouse. So full, only a narrow pathway to the kitchen existed.

Here, a beautifully carved headboard. There, a highboy. Here, a pair of wingback chairs. There, countless packing boxes. So many boxes. What was in the boxes? Every bibelot ever made?

Marjorie grinned at me from a clear spot on the stairs. "You're home."

"Am I?" I didn't recognize my house.

"They made it sound as if you expected them." It was as close to an apology as Marjorie ever came. She stood and took the car keys from my numb fingers. "I'll take care of Mother. You can deal with this." She waved her empty hand at my packed-to-the-gills house, then frowned. "What is this stuff?"

"Haven't the faintest."

She offered a better-you-than-me grin, squeezed past a tower of boxes, and escaped.

I crossed my fingers, squeezed my eyes shut, and hoped this

was a bad dream. I also hoped I'd wake up soon. But when I opened my eyes, the house still strained at its seams. "Aggie?" I called.

"Kitchen."

I took the now narrow path.

Boxes (each one marked "kitchen") were everywhere—stacked on the island, on the counters (where they encroached on Mr. Coffee's space), and on the floor. Aggie offered me a sympathetic grimace. "I got home as the movers left."

I held up my hands then let them drop. "Anarchy said his mother was sending a few things."

Aggie's dry chuckle made me wince. "This is more than a few things." She pointed at a box with a pair of scissors. "Should we open one?"

I nodded, and she slit through the packing tape, opened the box's flap, and peered inside.

"What's in there?"

She pulled out something wrapped in butcher's paper and handed it to me.

I unwrapped a stack of Wedgewood dinner plates. "Ventnor."

She tilted her head. "What do you mean?"

"The pattern is Ventnor." Bright fruit clustered in the plate's center and fruited garlands decorated the rim. It was lovely and old. I turned over the plate and studied the mark. "I'm guessing this set is from the 1920s."

"Pretty, but we don't need more fine china in this house."

I took in the vast number of boxes. "Do you think it's all china?"

"That and crystal."

"We don't need more crystal either. Why would Celeste send this?" A rhetorical question. My mother-in-law wanted to get rid of it. She'd sent a house's worth of antiques for me to deal with.

I'd never visited Celeste's house. I'd never been invited, and after the diatribe I was planning, I never would be. Given her granola vibe, I suspected she'd filled it with modern furniture or bean bags. I returned the plate to the open box. Celeste had no use for delicate china that needed to be hand-washed. I bet she used hand-thrown pottery plates and mugs.

"What do we do with this?" asked Aggie.

"They're family heirlooms. We'll need to go through everything with Anarchy."

"And in the meantime? Do you want to live like this?"

"No. I'll see if I can arrange for a storage unit." I planted my elbows on the counter and let my head drop to my hands.

Aggie put a full coffee cup in front of me.

"Thanks." I took a grateful sip. "Mac's truck is fixed?"

"Enough to get us home. How's your mother?"

"Bruised, but unbroken. Well, except for her left arm and leg. They're broken. She's cranky." Such an understatement.

She wrinkled her nose. "And Max?"

"Got into some cheese."

"Ah."

Ding, dong.

"I'll get it. You relax." Aggie weaved her way through the boxes, and I slumped onto a stool.

The back door swung open, and Grace froze. Her eyes grew wide. "What is all this?"

Max snuck past her legs and passed gas as he dashed into the family room.

I didn't have the energy to chase him down. Instead, I offered Grace a tired, throttling-my-mother-in-law-might-happen smile. "Celeste sent it."

"Gosh."

Not the four-letter word floating through my mind.

"What are you going to do?"

Crash.

The house shook, and I jumped from the stool. "Max!"

I raced into the family room (what was once the family room
—now it was a storage room for a Hepplewhite chest, a set of
Chippendale chairs, a pair of bachelor's chests, a waterfall bookcase, and ten thousand boxes stacked almost to the ceiling).

McCallester perched atop the highest stack, and Max circled
below.

They'd already knocked over one stack.

"Max. Bad dog."

He ignored me and passed more gas.

"Oh my God, Max. Gross." Grace waved at the smell (a futile
gesture since the whole house smelled like a garbage dumpster
on a hot day). Then she retreated a step. "I have to go. I just
came home to pick up my tennis racket, then I babysit." She
abandoned me.

I poked at an upholstered chair. Mint velvet. No one had
touched it since 1957.

"Ellison."

I turned and faced Aggie. "Yes?"

"A Mr. Lloyd Foster is here to see you."

I closed my eyes for a full ten seconds. "No."

"No?"

I peeked at Aggie. Her forehead creased and the expression
in her eyes was serious. She wasn't kidding.

"The house."

She didn't reply, but Max passed more gas, then lifted onto
his back paws, leaned his front paws against a stack of boxes
marked fragile, and growled.

"No!"

The stack wobbled.

Meow. McCallester voiced his discontent.

"Max!"

The boxes and McCallester hit the floor. If the sound was
any indication, they'd taken out a generation's worth of Cham-
pagne glasses. Neither cat nor dog gave the broken heirlooms a

second thought. The cat leapt onto the empty bookcase, and Max chased him.

"Max! Bad dog."

"Is everything quite all right?" Lloyd's plummy accent had me turning my head as Max expelled more gas.

I forced my horrified face into a welcoming expression. "Lloyd, how lovely to see you."

The cat made a hacking sound and vomited a hairball onto Anarchy's family heirloom.

McCallester's vomit and the scent of Max's gas combined to drive me from the room. I grabbed Lloyd's arm and pulled him into the kitchen. "I'm so sorry. You caught us in a bit of a mess." Not a bit. "Bit" suggested a tiny amount. This? This mess was epic.

"I'd offer to come back another time, but I'm only in Kansas City for a few hours."

I hid a grimace behind a polite smile. "My studio is upstairs."

"Wait." He nodded toward a painting of a salad. "Is that one of yours?"

"It is."

He grinned. "Lead the way. I can't wait to see more."

We'd climbed halfway to the second floor when the doorbell rang.

"Drat." I offered my guest a rueful smile. "Excuse me a moment." I descended and opened the door.

Prudence Davies pushed into my foyer. "You haven't returned my calls."

I didn't need to justify my failure to call Prudence, but decades of good manners overrode my desire to kick her out on her keister. "I'm sorry. I've been busy."

"My mother is dead." And Prudence was a viable suspect.

"My Mother is in the hospital."

Crash!

The house shook, Aggie swore. Colorfully. And McCallester streaked into the foyer with Max at his heels.

The cat ran under a chair.

Max ran smack into the chair, paused, then shook his head.

"Bad dog! Bad cat!"

The animals cared not one whit for my scolding. McCallester dashed up the stairs with Max close behind him.

I anticipated the disaster, and my shoulders tightened till they touched my ears. But anticipation didn't hold a candle to reality. McCallester dashed between Lloyd's legs, Max slammed into him, and the Englishman tottered. For a brief second, hope flamed in my chest. Lloyd made a desperate grab for the railing, but his fingers closed on air and he fell, end over end. He landed at the bottom of the stairs and didn't move.

I climbed over a chair to get to him. "Lloyd!"

"Your cat and dog killed him."

I ignored Prudence. "Aggie!" My voice resembled that of a wounded water buffalo.

Aggie came running.

"Ambulance!"

She turned on her heel and headed for the nearest phone.

"Is he dead?" asked Prudence from her spot near the door.

I shot her a murderous scowl, then focused on Lloyd. His chest rose and fell. He was alive. But the growing pool of blood beneath his head was terrifying. Should I try to staunch the bleeding? What if he had spinal injuries and moving his head made them worse?

I glared at the top of the stairs, where McCallester watched us with feline disinterest. Max saw the expression on my face and slunk away.

I knelt next to Lloyd, held his limp fingers, and made a promise. "Help is on the way."

Seconds later, Aggie bustled into the front hall. She shoved the chair that had slowed Max until it blocked the entrance to the living room, then she stacked boxes on top of its cushions.

"What are you doing?" I asked. Now was not the time to reorganize Anarchy's furniture.

"Making room for a gurney," Aggie replied.

Prudence picked up a box and carried it into the study.

When she emerged empty-handed, I repeated my question. "What are you doing?"

"Helping."

Somewhere, a large pink pig sprouted wings and soared through the sky.

The ambulance arrived quickly, and competent men wrapped Lloyd's neck in a foam collar, took his vitals, and loaded the unconscious Englishman onto a gurney.

"Please take him to St. Marks. My mother is already there." That earned me a raised eyebrow. "She didn't fall!" The entire downstairs was a tripping hazard. Throw in McCallester and Max, and it was a wonder any of us were still standing. "She had a car accident. Rear-ended. She broke her arm and leg. Oh, and she had internal injuries. There was a surgery. A long one—"

"Sure."

I wasn't certain if the EMT was agreeing to St. Mark's, or if he wanted to me to be quiet.

"I was with her this morning when all this—" I waved an arm at the packed foyer "—was delivered."

He nodded. Once. "You'll follow us there?" He didn't care about by my near-to-bursting house, just his patient.

"Will Lloyd be okay?"

"Head injuries are tricky." He made no promises. "You'll come to the hospital?"

"Yes." Except Marjorie had my car, and Grace and her car were long gone. "Aggie, may I borrow your car?"

"I'll take you," said Prudence.

What evil plot was she hatching? "No, thank you."

"It's no trouble."

"Mac has my car," said Aggie. "I loaned it to him while a local mechanic checks his truck."

"Can I ride in the ambulance?"

"Are you family?"

"No," I admitted.

"Sorry."

I swallowed a sigh (and my pride) and turned to Prudence. "I'd appreciate a ride."

She offered me a patently insincere smile. "It'll give us a chance to talk."

Oh joy.

We stepped onto the stoop and watched the ambulance disappear down the driveway, then I followed Prudence to her BMW and opened the passenger door.

She slid behind the wheel, inserted the key in the ignition, but didn't start the car.

I shifted in my seat. "We should go.

"I didn't kill my mother."

"Then I'm sure the police will find the real killer."

"I'm being framed."

This wasn't a movie or a cop show. Murderers didn't frame innocent women for their crimes. "Why would someone kill Muriel?" Also, why weren't we moving?

Prudence's hands tightened on the steering wheel, and she scowled out the windshield.

"We should go."

She huffed and turned the key.

I folded my hands on my lap and stared out the window. "Money."

I tore my gaze from my neighbors' landscaping. "Pardon?"

"Money. It's a motive."

"Don't you inherit everything?" Prudence was an only child.

"There's a large bequest to someone I've never heard of."

Did Anarchy and Peters know about this mysterious bequest? Was it even real? "Your theory is that this unknown heir murdered your mother and framed you for the crime?" I couldn't discount suspicions. Not entirely. After all, a pig had flown today.

"It's a possibility," she snapped.

Her theory seemed too convenient, but I had no desire to debate motives with her. "As you wish."

"Tell your husband I'm innocent."

Yesterday, if someone told me I'd be in Prudence's car as she requested a favor, I'd have called them nuts. Just being near her made my skin itch. Then again, her pinched lips and white knuckles suggested she wasn't thrilled by my presence.

I made a non-committal sound in the back of my throat.

"Is that a no?" Prudence jerked the car to the curb and glared at me.

"This isn't the hospital."

"I. Didn't. Kill. Her."

"You already said that."

"She needed more help than I could give her."

I said nothing.

"She forgot things. Simple things. She got confused. Often."

"I'm sorry."

"When I mentioned a nursing facility, she attacked me. Balled her hand into a fist and hit me in the jaw."

I'd have paid money to see that. "I'm sorry."

She exhaled, then slumped as if I were the one who'd socked her in the jaw. "You resent me."

Oh, please. "Wrong. I dislike you."

"Henry loved me."

Discussing my late husband's freely shared affections with one of his paramours was...beneath me. "If you say so."

"It's true."

If believing that gave her comfort, who was I to disagree? I shrugged.

"It's as if you don't care."

"About Henry's wandering eye? I don't. Are you planning on taking me to the hospital, or should I walk home and call a cab?"

Prudence growled, but she pulled back onto the road. "Who's the man who fell down the stairs?"

"Lloyd Foster."

"Why were you taking him upstairs?"

"To visit my studio. He wanted to see my work."

The corner of her lip curled into an unpleasant sneer. "Is that what artists call it?"

"Call what?"

"Taking men who aren't their husbands upstairs."

I gaped at her. Did she seriously think I'd cheat on Anarchy? "I thought you wanted a favor."

Her cheeks darkened. "I do."

"Then why insult me?"

Long seconds passed, and her forehead creased as if I'd asked a difficult question. "I can't help it."

It was like Aesop's fable about the scorpion and the frog. The scorpion asked the frog for a ride across a river. The frog was afraid of being stung and declined, but the scorpion argued that if it did so, they'd both drown. The frog agreed, but midway across the river, the scorpion stung. As the frog sank beneath the water, he asked, "Why?" The scorpion replied, "It's my nature."

Prudence was the scorpion with compulsions she couldn't repress even when it was in her best interest. Her unique compulsion was to insult me. Every chance she got. She simply couldn't help herself.

That made me the too-trusting frog.

Prudence pulled the car to a stop in front of the hospital, and I closed my fingers around the handle.

"You'll tell your husband?"

"I will."

"You'll tell him I'm innocent?"

"I'll tell him we talked. Thank you for the ride." Manners mattered. So did empathy. "I'm sorry about Muriel's memory loss. That couldn't have been easy."

She stared out the windshield and barely nodded. "It was awful, but I didn't kill her."

In that moment, I believed her. Of course, I did. I was the too-trusting frog.

CHAPTER NINE

I pushed through the hospital's revolving door, paused in the crowded lobby, and took a moment to gather my thoughts.

In less than a day, Mother had endured a near-fatal car accident, I'd managed what felt like five minutes of sleep, my house became a warehouse, and, thanks to Max and McCallester, a man I'd hoped to impress had tumbled down my stairs like Humpty-Dumpty. Oh, and Prudence Davies had tried to convince me of her innocence. Before I braved the ER and the you-again smirk on the admitting nurse's face. I needed a moment. How long would it take to order to-go coffee?

Around me, visitors peered through the gift shop window, checked their watches, and stood in line for a table at the coffee shop.

I eyed the line, and my sigh rose from the depths of my soul. Too long. I couldn't in good conscience linger when Lloyd was in the ER.

Turning away from the coffee shop, I bumped into someone. "I'm so sorr—Connie, what happened?"

Connie's right arm was strapped to her body. At my question, her cheeks flushed. "I tripped over my dog and broke my collarbone."

"There's a lot of that going around." That sounded less than sympathetic. "How awful for you."

She grimaced. "It wasn't Gigi's fault. I didn't see her."

"Gigi?"

"Our miniature poodle. Poof. She appeared beneath my feet."

"Dogs can be sneaky that way." Or they could barrel into unsuspecting victims like a runaway locomotive.

She nodded her agreement. "But what would we do without them?" She pressed a hand to her lips, and her eyes swam with tears.

"Was Gigi hurt?"

"No. Thank heavens, she's fine." Connie swallowed. "I didn't get a chance to tell you after the meet, my congratulations to Grace. She swam well."

"Thank you. I'll tell her you said so. Laine won her races?" It wasn't really a question. I'd been there.

"She did. About the meet. I wasn't myself. It was hot and crowded." She rubbed a hand across her face, erasing a tear. "But that's no excuse. I had no call to be so awful."

"We all have off days."

"I guess so. What brings you here?"

"A guest in my home tripped over my dog."

"You're kidding."

"I wish." I glanced at her taped arm. "Are you coming or going?"

"Going?"

"Is your husband picking you up?" Driving with an arm strapped to her chest had to be difficult.

"No." Her clipped tone discouraged further comment.

"I'd offer to take you, but I caught a ride myself."

"I'll be fine. I drove down here."

"I should get to the ER." I nodded at her collarbone. "I hope you feel better soon."

"Ellison."

I recognized the voice and turned. Anarchy stood at the hospital's entrance, and he wore a thunderous expression.

"Excuse me, Connie." I hurried to Anarchy's side. "You're here." How? Why? And what was up with his angry frown?

"Aggie called. She said you'd left the house with a murder suspect." That didn't sound like something Aggie would do.

"It was just Prudence."

Behind me, Connie gasped. Perfect. That gossip would be all over town by cocktail hour.

Anarchy, realizing we'd been overheard, held out his hand and served up his most charming smile. "Anarchy Jones. I don't believe we've had the pleasure."

Connie opened her mouth, but no words came out. He'd dazzled away her ability to talk.

I tugged on his sleeve. "We should get to the ER and check on Lloyd."

"Of course. Nice meeting you, Connie."

Still mute, she nodded.

When I glanced over my shoulder, she was watching us walk away.

"Aggie called to tell you I'd caught a ride with Prudence?"

"Aggie called to tell me Lloyd fell. Then she said Marjorie had your car, and you'd caught a ride with Prudence. She didn't see the danger."

I didn't either. "That makes two of us."

His lips thinned. "You got in a car with a woman who may have killed her mother and put yours in the hospital. Not smart."

My back stiffened. I wasn't accustomed to being patronized by anyone but Mother. I didn't like it when Mother did it. I especially didn't like it when my husband did it. My feet slowed, and Anarchy walked a few steps ahead of me.

When he realized he was walking alone, he turned. "What?"

"I'm not an idiot."

"I didn't say you were."

"You kind of did."

"I worry."

"That doesn't mean you can speak to me like that." I was standing up for myself. Perhaps if I'd done more of that during my first marriage, I wouldn't have spent seventeen years with a man I didn't love. I did love Anarchy. But if our marriage was going to work, we needed to respect each other. "I worry too, but I don't speak to you as if you're a naughty child."

He stared at me, his face unreadable.

I resisted the urge to cross my arms, make a face, and prove his point. Instead I returned his gaze and stood firm.

A hospital corridor probably wasn't the best place for this discussion. But sometimes life sneaks up on you, and you have to ignore the adrenaline rush that says *flight*! You have to stand your ground, or you'll be running forever. That, or you'll be run over.

The hard expression in his eyes softened. "You're right."

I blinked.

"I'm sorry."

I released a breath I hadn't realized I was holding. "You're forgiven."

He closed the distance between us and wrapped me in his arms.

I rested my forehead against his chest and breathed easier.

"What happened to Lloyd?"

I tilted my head so I could see his eyes. "The animals knocked him down the stairs."

He winced and took my hand. "I hope we have good home-owner's insurance.

"The best." I made a mental note to call my—our—agent, Jack Billings.

"Probably wise."

Given the regular disasters at our house, over-insuring was definitely wise. I said as much.

He rewarded me with a chuckle, and we entered the ER and approached the admitting nurse.

"Mrs. Russell." Her voice was a sigh. And not a happy-to-see-you kind of sigh. More like an I'm-at-the-end-of-my-rope-and you're-back sigh.

"It's Jones now. A Mr. Lloyd Foster arrived via ambulance."

"Are you family?"

"No. But he was injured in my home."

"I can't let you back there."

"I'm aware." I was intimately familiar with the ER rules. "Perhaps the doctor can step out and speak with us?"

"I'll ask." Her response was grudging. She pushed away from her desk and disappeared into the treatment area.

"Have you been home?" I asked.

"No."

"Celeste sent—"

"Aggie told me. I'm sorry. How much is there?"

"We could furnish a second house."

"Wow." He shoved his hands into his pockets. "Mother stored it in California. We could store it here."

I sank onto a chair.

"Or..."

I looked up at him. "Or?"

"We could buy a vacation house."

"Where?"

"Do you like to ski?"

I nodded.

"Or the beach? Do you like the beach?"

"Yes."

"You don't seem excited by the idea."

"When you have a vacation house, that's where you go on vacation."

"And you'd rather visit different places."

"Unless you want an Italian villa. But that wouldn't solve our furniture problem. We're not shipping that much furniture to Italy. I propose we go through everything, incorporate your favorite pieces, and store the rest."

"For how long?"

"Until Grace needs to furnish an apartment or house."

He rubbed his chin. "Not a bad idea."

"Mrs. Jones?"

I stood.

"I'm Dr Cuthbert." The doctor looked to be just older than Grace.

"You're new."

He blinked behind round John Lennon glasses that made his pale blue eyes enormous.

"I know most everyone in the department," I explained.

Dr. Cuthbert blinked again.

"I was Ellison Russell."

His gaze flickered. "I might have heard that name."

"I bet. How's Mr. Foster?"

"A laceration that required five stitches and a mild concussion. We'll keep him overnight for observation."

Anarchy held out his hand. "I'm Mr. Jones. Can we see him?"

The doctor shook Anarchy's hand. "He's being transferred to a room now." He gave us the room number, offered me a polite nod, and returned to his patients.

"Shall we visit your mother while the nurses get Lloyd settled?"

"I haven't finished her list." A list that required stopping at her house for pillows, a bed jacket, her address book, and stationery. Also making multiple phone calls and running a handful of errands.

"You've been busy."

"Mother doesn't accept excuses."

He grinned. "If you can stand up to me when I'm being unreasonable, you can do the same to her."

I searched his face. He was serious.

"I really am sorry I spoke to you like that. Worry took over." His hands closed on my shoulders. "I've finally found the woman of my dreams. I refuse to lose her."

"You're stuck with me."

He brushed the pads of his fingers down my cheek. "Promise me you won't take unnecessary risks."

"Likewise?"

He pursed his lips. He was a cop. I was an artist. He was supposed to take risks. I was supposed to paint pretty pictures.

My lungs deflated. "Speaking of danger. I'll brave the lion's den if you'll run to the gift shop and buy flowers for Lloyd."

"I have a better offer. I'll visit your mother. You buy the flowers."

"You mean it?"

"I do."

"You'd do that for me?"

"I would."

"I knew there was a reason I married you."

He waggled his brows. "Hopefully that reason is not the way I talk to your mother."

I smirked, and he caught my arm and pulled me close. "Need a reminder about that reason?"

"Tonight." I lifted on my toes, kissed his cheek, and took off for the gift shop before he changed his mind about Mother.

I collected a variety of magazines, the local paper, a couple of paperback books, and paused in front of the glass fronted cooler. My flower choices were daisies, lilies, or carnations arranged to look like ice cream in a sundae glass.

"Shopping for your mother?"

I turned and smiled at Shirley Davidson who held a Boston fern. "Actually, no. A guest fell down the stairs at my house."

"How awful. Not too serious, I hope."

"He'll be fine."

"How is your mother?"

"Cra—" telling Shirley that Mother was cranky might be the ticket to an early grave "—grateful to be alive. She broke her arm and leg."

"That's what I heard. So terrible the car didn't stop."

"Terrible," I agreed. "You were on my call list. Mother and Daddy will need to reschedule dinner."

"Don't give it a thought. Frances and I will put something on the calendar when she's feeling better." She eyed the flowers in the cooler. "Tough decision."

"Daisies are too casual," I replied.

"And lilies too funereal."

"And the carnations are for a child."

"A potted plant?" she suggested.

"He doesn't live in Kansas City."

"Oh?" Her gaze was speculative.

"How's Sabra?" My question wiped away the speculation.

"Fine. You heard?"

I offered the tiniest shrug. "People talk."

She huffed her agreement. "It was such a stupid thing to do."

"Love makes fools of us all."

"Shakespeare?"

"Thackery."

Shirley caught her lower lip in her teeth and shook her head. "If she'd only done as we expected. How foolish can one girl be? A bartender? I don't care if he does have Kansas City connections."

That was new. "He has Kansas City connections?"

Shirley turned the color of hospital mashed potatoes. Pale. And gluey. And somehow lumpy.

"May I help you?" asked an older woman in a pale blue smock.

I shifted my focus to the volunteer who'd interrupted. "Are these the only flowers in stock?"

"Yes."

"Perhaps some candy." I turned back to Shirley, but she'd slipped away, leaving me with the woman with bad timing. I tamped down a sigh. "Do you have any good chocolate?"

The volunteer, who'd sprayed her wispy hair into a blueish-gray beehive and painted her eyelids a sparkly turquoise, nodded toward a display of Russell Stover's.

Boxed chocolate was a dangerous proposition. You never knew when you'd bite into vile strawberry fluff. "Do you have the boxes with just nuts?"

"In the back."

I purchased the reading material and chocolate then hurried to rescue Anarchy from the lion's den.

I'd been to cocktail parties less crowded than Mother's hospital room. Daddy, Anarchy and Marjorie were joined by Shirley, Ellen Whitfield, Lydia Cockburn, Patience Murrow, and a nurse whose fussing about too many visitors was roundly ignored.

Anarchy offered me a relieved smile.

"Did you bring my pillow?" asked Mother.

I glanced at the small paper sack in my left hand. "I haven't had time."

"What do you need, Frannie?" Daddy looked better today, more grounded and stronger now that he knew Mother would recover.

"A few things from the house."

"Why didn't you ask me?"

"Ellison doesn't mind."

"Neither do I."

"Harrington, let the girls run the errands. You stay here with me."

Daddy looked as if he might argue. After all, grabbing a pillow from their bed hardly put him out, but I gave my head a tiny shake. There was no need to antagonize Mother. Not when she was already cranky.

"Ellen, Lydia, Patience, how nice to see you."

Mother's friends offered me sympathetic smiles.

Anarchy edged toward the door. "Harrington, I'll stop by tonight."

I raised my brows.

"Your husband is setting up a bed in the family room," Daddy explained.

Mother sniffed her disapproval.

"Frannie, the doctor said no stairs."

"It's ridiculous, I—"

"Have you given more thought to who hit you?" asked Anarchy.

"It was an accident," Mother replied.

He'd done it. He'd headed off a rant. "I'm not convinced."

"Well then, it was a mistake. Someone thought Ellison was driving my car."

So I was the target? "I never drive your car."

"But you do get targeted by killers."

Mother's friends watched us with fascinated expressions on their faces.

"Anarchy, we should check on Lloyd."

He joined me in the short ell that led to the hallway. We were almost free.

"Mother, I'll see you soon."

"You're leaving already?"

Guilt tickled at my throat then slid south to coil in my stomach.

Three words. Three. Words. And Mother made it clear I didn't care that she lay in a hospital bed.

"I'll be back. Soon." My attempt to placate her was like trying to repair a shattered Ming vase with school glue. A sad, futile effort.

Her friends' faces tightened in judgment.

"A man fell down the stairs at our house," I explained. "He's been hospitalized. We need to visit him."

"You're putting a stranger over family." Mother's long-suffering tone suggested I'd just delivered her a death blow.

"When the stranger might sue me? I think my family can do without me for thirty minutes."

"Go on, sugar," said Daddy. "Marjorie and I will keep your mother company."

I produced a brittle smile, and Anarchy and I escaped.

We were halfway to the elevator when Anarchy spoke. "We left your father with a coven."

I shrugged. "Daddy can handle that bunch." After all, he lived with Mother.

"Do Shirley Davidson & Patience Murrow dislike each other?"

"Not that I'm aware. Why?"

"Shirley dropped her Boston fern when she spotted Patience."

"Patience is Muriel Jarret's sister-in-law, and they never got along. But other than Muriel, everyone seems to like Patience."

"Unusual to have a Patience and a Prudence in the same family."

"I think Patience's mother was Charity."

"Got it."

"I can't throw stones." I'd named my daughter Grace. "You're sure Shirley reacted to Patience?"

"She made a face." He demonstrated by narrowing his eyes, wrinkling his nose and drawing his lips away from his teeth.

"Wow. She held it?"

"No. And I'm not sure anyone but me noticed. They focused on the fern falling to the floor."

"I'll ask Mother when she's in a better mood." Which might be next year. "How did you get roped into setting up a bed?"

"I offered."

"Thank you. Daddy will need all the help he can get."

"Your mother's a bad patient?"

"The worst. She hates not being in charge."

We rode the elevator up one floor and stepped into the corridor.

"Any ideas what we should say to Lloyd?"

"Beside an abject apology? McCallester ran through his legs. Max ran into him."

"Ouch."

"There was blood."

"Bring him a painting. As a gift."

"That's not a bad idea."

"Tell him we'll pay his medical bills."

I nodded.

"Bring him dinner from Winstead's." Anarchy had a weakness for steakburgers and onion rings.

"Good idea."

We paused in front of Lloyd's door, and I took a deep breath. This was the hospital room where I should feel guilt. Poor Lloyd had come to look at paintings, and our pets sent him careening down the stairs. "Let's do this."

"Hold on." Anarchy took the pager from his belt and frowned. "It can wait."

"Can it?"

"You're more important."

My heart fluttered, and we pushed through the door.

Lloyd sat in the hospital bed with a bandage on his head and a frown on his face. The frown disappeared when he saw us.

"Lloyd, I am so sorry."

He waved away my apology. "Don't be silly, my dear. I'll dine out on this for years."

I advanced a step. "Can you forgive us?"

"Forgiven and forgotten if you come to London next summer for a show."

A show? "You didn't see my studio."

"I saw the salad."

"The salad?" asked Anarchy.

"The painting in the kitchen," Lloyd replied. "Your wife has a great talent. Some artists paint beauty. Ellison takes pain or anger or sadness and makes it beautiful."

He got all that from a salad? I approached Lloyd's bedside. "We brought you books and magazines and chocolate."

Lloyd caught my wrist as I put my offerings on the table next to the bed. "Say you'll come to London."

Anarchy and I exchanged a quick glance, then I looked into Lloyd's dilated eyes and said, "We'd be delighted."

CHAPTER TEN

I gazed at the oatmeal-hued walls as Anarchy spoke into a payphone. Why did hospitals choose such wretched colors? A simple cream showed too much dirt? An actual beige was too bold a choice? A soft blue would clash with their terrible art? More pressing questions demanded my attention. Like Mother's demands. First stop, Mother and Daddy's where I'd pick up her pillow and bedjacket and address book. Then I needed to inventory my studio. The canvases for my upcoming show in Chicago were nearly finished. After that, I'd need to paint like a dervish to be ready for the show in London. Then the house. What stayed and what went to storage? I leaned against the wall in anticipatory exhaustion. I even closed my eyes.

"They found the Mark III."

I opened my eyes and stared at my husband.

"The one that hit Mother? Where?"

"A home not far from yours. It belongs to Millicent and Martin French."

"They're in Europe."

Anarchy rubbed the back of his neck. "How do you know they're in Europe?"

"Everyone knows they're in Europe. Millie spent six months planning this trip. She grilled me about which museums to visit in Italy and France. Three times. How did they find the car?"

"Their next-door neighbor called about the strange car parked behind the house."

"So, if the neighbor didn't call—"

"The car might have gone undiscovered till they returned home," said Anarchy.

"They're not due back till the end of July, but I'm sure the cleaning lady or the lawn service would notice a wrecked car behind the house."

"But would they call it in?"

"It depends on whether they're in the US legally."

Anarchy frowned. "Do you mind if we stop on our way home?"

"Of course not."

Which is how I ended up perched on the stone wall circling the French's back patio as Anarchy and Peters circled a baby blue Mark III with front end damage. "Is it Muriel's?"

"Yes," Anarchy replied

Who would steal a car, then park it four blocks from its home garage? No one. Who would wreck a car and hide it at an empty-for-six-weeks house? Prudence. "Why would Prudence crash into Mother?"

"Prudence Davies isn't exactly a fan. Of you, or your mother."

Not a fan? That was putting it mildly. Depending on the day, Prudence either disliked me or hated me with the intensity of ten thousand suns. But her antipathy was nothing new. If she were planning vehicular homicide (look at me with the police jargon), why now?

I shifted so the rock jabbing my derriere was less painful.

"She was already a suspect in her own mother's murder. Why go after mine?" Try as I might, I couldn't imagine a motive.

"If we arrested her, she might not get another chance."

So Prudence was suddenly a homicidal maniac? "Maybe it was an accident. Then she panicked." Even as I said the words, I doubted them. Prudence wasn't the type of woman who panicked.

Anarchy wiped a bead of sweat from his brow. "Maybe."

The sun glinted off the car, and I was grateful for my spot in the shade. The humidity turned temperatures in the upper eighties into one hundred twenty degrees. At least. Even Peters had shed his ubiquitous raincoat. He wore a short sleeve sport shirt and studied the Mark III's front grill as if there might be a test on mangled metal.

He noticed me watching and the lip beneath his unfortunate mustache curled. Then, as if he'd suddenly remembered I'd married his partner, he produced a sickly smile. "How's McCallester?"

Nothing but trouble. "He and Max are at odds." And they were destroying Anarchy's family's heirlooms at an exponential rate.

Peters grunted. "It was nice having him around."

I glanced at Anarchy. How attached to the cat was he? Grace rescued McCallester then gave him to Anarchy. When Anarchy and I married, McCallester returned to my home—our home. Thus far, his second time living in my—our—house was an even bigger disaster than the first time. "Maybe he could come for a visit."

Peters straightened and joined Anarchy in peering into the car's front seat.

"Anarchy, would you mind?" I asked.

"Mind what?"

"If McCallester stayed with Peters for a few days."

"No."

"Wonderful. It's settled. We'll bring him by tonight."

Peters opened his mouth to argue.

A trickle of sweat crawled down my back. "I think he misses you, detective."

Peters' mouth snapped shut.

Anarchy shot me an amused glance then opened the car door and took a giant step back.

No surprise there. The Mark III was parked in the sun, and opening the passenger door had to be like opening a blast furnace.

"Where's Rollins?" Peters groused.

"Who's Rollins?" I asked.

"The fingerprint guy."

Muriel's fingerprints would be all over the car. Probably Prudence's. Were they looking for someone else's? "Do you have other suspects? Besides Prudence, I mean."

"She claimed the car was stolen," Anarchy replied.

"And you believed her?"

Peters chuckled.

"You're right. It'd be easy to report the car stolen then stash it here. Everyone knows Millie and Martin went to Europe." His lips quirked, and his brown eyes were probably twinkling behind his aviator glasses' dark lenses.

I glanced back at the French's house, a stone, brick and stucco English Tudor. Every blind was drawn, and the plants missed by the sprinkler system wilted in the heat. The place looked obviously empty.

A young man rounded the corner of the house. He carried a case in his right hand and leaned to the left to counter the case's weight, but when he spotted Anarchy and Peters, he straightened. "The whole car?"

"Pay special attention to the handles, the steering wheel, and the dash."

This must be Rollins. I hopped off the wall and extended my hand. "I'm Ellison Jones."

"Nice to meet you." He dropped his case on the drive, opened it, and pulled out a pair of gloves. Then he shook my hand. "You'd be surprised by the number of people who forget to wipe the underside of the door handle."

"I'd never think of that."

He nodded as if I'd made his point, then pulled on his gloves.

"Are you ready?" asked Anarchy.

As much as I wanted to watch Rollins at work, I wanted air-conditioning more. "Sure."

Anarchy nodded to Peters. "I'll take Ellison home and catch up with you at the station."

Peters grunted.

Anarchy and I returned to the street where he'd parked in the shade of a dying elm. "If Prudence was driving when the car hit your mother, she could park here and walk home." He turned the ignition, but rather than pull away from the curb, he tilted his head and closed his eyes.

"What does your gut say?"

"My gut? She didn't do it. Peters disagrees."

They were at an impasse, and I fell firmly on Anarchy's side. But what if he was wrong? "She had a sudden vendetta against ladies of a certain age?"

"It's why I worried when you drove with her. If I'm wrong, if Prudence is killing people, you'd be high on her list."

I couldn't argue with that. "Even if Prudence did kill her mother—" I adjusted the vent till cold air blasted straight at me "—why go after mine?"

"Sometimes motives aren't clear."

My shiver had nothing to do with the air conditioning.

"Jones!" Peters ran down the driveway, waving his arms like a madman. "We need you."

"I can take you home first."

"Peters is just starting to like me." Not really. "Don't make him wait on my account. I'll walk home."

His hand hovered near the door handle. "You're sure?"

"Positive. Go." I exited the car, grateful I lived in a neighborhood with mature trees. Their shade made the heat bearable.

My sandals weren't made for walking, and a blister formed between my toes. I ignored the pain and ambled my way home. It gave me time to think.

Was Prudence a killer?

Much as I disliked her, I couldn't imagine she'd suffocate her own mother. If Prudence didn't kill Muriel, then who? The recipient of that mysterious bequest?

No easy answer presented itself, and my thoughts drifted to the furniture crammed into my house.

That problem required an immediate solution. The kitchen was too crowded for Aggie to cook. There was no serene spot to relax with a cup of coffee or a cocktail. No place to watch the evening news.

I lifted damp hair from the back of my neck and turned onto my block.

Libba had parked her red convertible in my drive.

I trudged up the driveway, and the front door opened.

Libba rested her hands on her hips, and her gaze took in my limp linen dress, my sweat-dampened hair, and my limp. "Your hostas look good."

I made a soft noise in my throat. Henry's murder had been hard on my plants. This summer, they'd rebounded.

"I hear you've been busy. How's Frances?"

"Demanding." Three steps from air-conditioning.

"But she'll be okay?"

"Full recovery." I hadn't spared my mother a single thought as I walked home.

"I have an idea."

My shoulders tensed. Libba's ideas often led to trouble. I needed air-conditioning before I listened. "Yes?"

Unfortunately, Libba blocked the door. "Loan all this furniture to Charlie." Charlie, Libba's current beau and my high-school boyfriend, had returned to Kansas City after an ugly divorce. He'd bought an enormous house and furnished it with a recliner, a card table and folding chairs, a television, and a bed.

"The furniture belongs to Anarchy."

"You can't even see what you have."

That was true. "I'll have to ask him."

"You can't live like this. Call him."

"He's not in his office."

"Where is he?"

"The Frenches' house."

"They're in Europe."

"I know."

She stepped fully outside, closed the door behind her, and dug in her purse. "C'mon."

My dream of cooling off in air-conditioning disappeared. "Where?"

"The Frenches'. You can't live like this."

"You already said that."

"It bears repeating. If there were a fire, you'd never make it out." She opened the driver's side door. "Get in."

Libba had the top down on her car. No air-conditioning. No iced coffee. "But—"

"No buts. Get in."

I hesitated. I desperately wanted air-conditioning. And iced coffee. Or Tab. And Anarchy was busy with Peters' discovery. He didn't have time to discuss furniture.

A blue Mercedes zipped up the drive and parked behind Libba. Jinx exited the car and marched toward us. "I tried calling."

"Busy morning," I replied.

"How's Frances?"

"She'll be fine." I might melt into a puddle of goo in the relentless sunshine, but Mother would be fine.

"You're sure? You look like hell."

"Gee, thanks." I felt like hell.

"I heard Prudence hit her."

"From whom?"

"Around." Jinx seldom revealed her sources.

"I'm taking Ellison to see Anarchy. He's at Millie and Martin's."

Jinx frowned. "They're in Europe." Then she speared me with her sharp gaze. "Do you think Prudence did it?"

"Why would she?

Jinx nodded as if I'd passed a secret test. "Especially now."

"You mean since she's already a suspect in her mother's murder?"

"That too."

"Why now, Jinx?"

"It's possible Prudence finally found an unmarried man." She held up a warning finger. "That is unsubstantiated gossip."

"Who?" Libba demanded. "The woman looks like Mr. Ed. Someone, explain to me how old horse-teeth attracts men."

"Maybe she met the right one." Jinx returned her focus to me. "What exactly happened to Frances?"

"She was rear-ended and pushed into traffic where her car was t-boned."

"And we don't know who rear-ended her?"

"Hit and run."

"Word is it was Muriel Jarret's Mark III."

"You should consider a career in law enforcement."

"Was it Muriel's car?"

"Prudence reported it stolen."

Jinx gave me a when-pigs-fly face, complete with slightly

twisted, pursed lips, lowered brows, and a tilt to her well-coiffed head.

"Why would Prudence hit Mother?"

"Are we going?" Libba demanded. "It's hot out here."

I was aware.

Anarchy pulled into the drive and parked behind Jinx. "Ladies."

Libba fixed a bulldog stare on him. "I have an idea."

"Oh?" The sun reflected off his sunglasses' lenses.

My lawn needed a shade tree. A big one. I wiped sweat from my brow and edged toward the front door.

"Loan the furniture to Charlie."

Anarchy looked my way, but I couldn't manage so much as a shrug. I was too hot, too tired, and too in need of coffee to form a single opinion.

"That's fine," he told her. "Libba, Jinx, Ellison will call you later." Then he took my arm and led me into the house.

The sudden chill on my skin was almost as good as diving into a swimming pool. I sighed in relief.

"Wow." Anarchy ignored the air-conditioning and stared open-mouthed at the crowded foyer. A few hours' absence hadn't made the stacks of boxes any shorter.

"Where did it all come from?" I asked.

"I'll have to look, but I assume my grandmother."

"I can't believe your sister or brother didn't want it."

"They did."

Meaning we got the leftovers.

"Is there furniture for a study?"

"Undoubtedly."

"We should keep that. Get rid of Henry's desk. Let Charlie borrow the rest."

"Fine. Whatever makes it go away fastest."

The door opened behind us, and Marjorie stepped inside. "Tag, you're it."

Already? I sighed. "Maybe a glass of iced coffee first."

"She's waiting for you."

"Coffee first, then the dratted pillow and the bedjacket. How does she think she'll get it over her cast? And I don't know why she needs stationery at the hospital."

Marjorie lifted a brow. "Do you want to argue with her?"

Decidedly not. "I guess the rest of my day is planned."

"Sit with her for a few hours, then we'll switch." My sister cut her gaze to Anarchy. "You must think we're terrible, negotiating who sits with our mother in the hospital."

"Not. At. All." His gaze took in the bursting foyer. "Mothers can be a challenge."

I walked into the hospital carrying Mother's pillow and an alligator overnight case packed with a bedjacket, her toothbrush, hairbrush and hairspray (nearly dying was no excuse for mussed hair), her address book, a box of engraved stationery, and the book from her bedside table.

Mother's room looked and smelled like a florist's shop.

"Where have you been?" she asked.

I smiled at Daddy who sat in the chair next to her bed. "They found the Mark III. It belonged to Muriel."

"So Prudence is guilty," he replied.

"She did say the car was stolen."

"Muriel was an angry, mean woman. Open the case on the bed, Ellison."

I put the overnight bag on the bed. "Muriel has an alibi."

Daddy stood. "I'll let you gals talk while I stretch my legs. Do you need anything, Frannie?"

"A frosty."

Daddy grinned and escaped.

I stood next to the plate-glass window. Outside, the sun shone (too brightly), birds soared, flowers bloomed, and children laughed. Here, in Mother's hospital room, ire tainted the air.

"The doctor says I can't go home." Mother was displeased.

"You had major surgery. I bet they'd like to keep an eye on you for one more day." Although, if I asked the nurses, I bet they'd send Mother home in a New York minute.

"Ellison."

I turned away from the view.

"Tell the doctor I'll be fine."

"Maybe you should listen to him."

"You and your father are being ridiculous." Hopefully that chocolate frosty would sweeten Mother's disposition.

"One more day, Mother."

She sniffed. "Where's Grace?"

"Babysitting." Grace had spent last evening with her grandmother and come home pale beneath her tan.

"Where's your sister?"

"Running your errands." Errands that included taking Mother's mink to Gerhardt's for storage, delivering her new linen napkins to be monogrammed, and returning a pair of shoes to Swanson's.

"Everyone brings me books." She scowled at the stack next to her bed. "I can't hold a book. And television? Who has time to watch the drivel they put on during the day?"

"Not me."

Either she missed the dryness of my tone or she ignored it.

"Sit. I can't bear your looming above me."

I sat.

The swelling on Mother's face had subsided, but the purple bruises had deepened to an imperial shade.

"I know you have things you'd rather be doing."

My house was a disaster. I had not one, but two upcoming shows. I'd spoken no more than a handful of words to Grace since Mother's accident. And I had a new husband. But I'd rue the day I mentioned any of those entirely valid reasons to be away from her. But, for all her bullying and bossing and berating, she was still my mother. And right now, she needed an assurance there was nothing I'd rather do than sit in her hospital room. "Don't be silly. There's no place I'd rather be." There was at least a grain of truth in that statement.

"You're a terrible liar."

I rubbed the tip of my nose then grinned. "I'm not lying. I expect Grace to show up when I'm in the hospital. You shouldn't expect less from me."

"You were always the one who met our expectations."

I wasn't sure if she'd complimented or insulted me. "Oh?"

"Marjorie was too wild. No sense of duty. But you? You behaved. I knew you'd marry the right man."

"Look how well that turned out."

"Grace."

Grace was worth every miserable minute with Henry. "Fair point."

"Then you rebelled. With a paint brush. It should have been a nice hobby. You didn't have to make it a job."

"Painting was how I dealt with an unhappy marriage."

"And now that you're happy?" Mother admitted that I was happy?

"My paintings may change."

"You've changed." She weighted her words with so much disapproval, they became an accusation.

"You have, too."

"Me?" The ghost of a smile touched her lips. "Never."

"Karma." Not cosmic balance, but my illegitimate half-sister (from before Mother married Daddy). She'd rocked Mother's world. But Mother rallied. I'd even heard her defending Karma.

She sniffed.

"You're almost blasé when I find a body."

"Jimmy Kline."

"Who?"

"Jimmy Kline. He's a friend of your father. The man can't

play golf. No short game. None. He can drive the ball a country mile, but put his ball in a bunker or deep rough, or give him a putt of more than three feet, and he's hopeless."

Had Mother sustained an undiagnosed head injury? "Should I call a nurse?"

"You should listen to your elders."

I'd wait on the nurse. "Fine."

"Jimmy spent countless hours on the practice putting green. Spent days up to his ankles in sand. And his game never improved. No. Short. Game."

"Your point?"

"He had to accept what he couldn't change. Now he plays scrambles. They almost always use his tee shot."

"I'm missing the point."

"I can't stop you from finding bodies. I might as well accept it."

"I don't find bodies on purpose."

"Most people don't find bodies at all."

I had no response.

"I worry. If it were Grace finding dead people, you'd worry." She made a good point.

I mumbled.

"What?"

"Nothing."

"Not only do you find bodies, you catch killers." She made that sound like a crime worse than murder.

I concentrated on my new wedding band. Simple. Gold. Classic. "Strictly speaking, Anarchy catches the killers."

"Don't be smart, Ellison." She turned her head my way. "Do you think someone tried to kill me?"

Was that a shimmer in her eyes?

"I don't know."

"Your best guess."

"Yes."

"Prudence?"

"It makes sense, but why?"

"Maybe she's wanted me dead for a long time and finally saw an opportunity."

"Maybe," I allowed. But that answer felt wrong. "She has no motive."

"Did she kill her mother?"

"There she has a motive."

Mother winced. "Money? Or because Muriel was a nightmare of a woman?"

"Could be either. Was Muriel always so awful?"

"Not when we were children. She was older than me, but I remember her. A free spirit."

How had a free-spirited child become a cane-wielding crone? "What happened?"

"No idea. Patience or Sally might know."

"I get the impression Patience loathed her."

"True." Mother gave a short nod. "She didn't think Muriel was good enough for her big brother. By all accounts, Muriel's marriage was...rocky."

Tap, tap. A doctor stuck his head in the room.

Mother somehow managed to look down her nose while lying in bed. "Ellison, give us a minute."

She didn't have to tell me twice. I escaped.

CHAPTER ELEVEN

*W*aking up next to Anarchy ranked with coffee as my favorite part of the morning. I stretched, languorous like McCallester in a pool of sunshine, then I turned toward my husband and found an empty bed.

Drat.

At least there was coffee. I threw on a robe, descended the front stairs, and navigated through furniture till I reached the kitchen. Mercifully someone had cleared a path to the coffee pot.

Good morning. Mr. Coffee's pot was full. *How are you?*

I poured a mug, then added cream. "Better now."

He offered a sympathetic grimace. *What will you do about this stuff?* Boxes, so many boxes, still crowded the kitchen.

I suspected Mr. Coffee wanted to use a stronger word than stuff but was too polite to swear in front of a woman.

"Libba is handling it."

Libba? You're sure that's a good idea? Mr. Coffee didn't usually second-guess. It was one of his many charms.

"She's moving everything to Charlie's. He needs furniture, and we have plenty. It's a long-term loan." If Libba took every stick of furniture, the house would still overflow with boxes. And I doubted Charlie wanted thirty-six place settings of floral china that required hand-washing.

Dr. Ardmore doesn't mind?

"Charlie's so busy practicing medicine and keeping Libba happy he may not notice."

What are you doing today?

I took an enormous gulp. "Taking Lloyd Foster to the airport, then spending time with Mother."

More coffee? It was as if he sensed my reluctance to spend hours sitting at the hospital while Mother barked at the nurses. That, or he knew my mug was near-empty.

I refilled, rested against the counter, and breathed deep.

Brnng, brnng.

I glanced at the clock. Eight fifteen. Too early for social calls. "Mother probably has a mile-long to-do list." One that couldn't wait till nine. I took a bracing gulp.

Brnng, brnng.

You could ignore it. No judgment. Another reason I adored Mr. Coffee.

"She'll just call again." Swallowing a sigh, I picked up the receiver. "Jones residence."

"Ellison?"

"This is she."

"It's Connie Jackson." A near breathless Connie Jackson. "Is it true?"

"Is what true?"

"Did the police issue an arrest warrant for Prudence?"

My heart thumped an extra beat, and I put down my mug and pressed my palm to my heart. "Connie, I just rolled out of bed. I haven't heard a thing."

"But your husband—"

"Doesn't discuss confidential police business with me." Not

strictly true, but he definitely didn't want me sharing confidences. And in this case, I was truly in the dark. So annoying.

"Well, the police are looking for her. Someone in uniform banged on her front door this morning." Connie's source was one of Prudence's neighbors.

Why hadn't Anarchy told me? What had Peters found in Muriel's car? I'd been too tired and overwhelmed to ask. Now I faced regrets. "I'm completely in the dark."

"I assumed you'd be interested."

My lips flattened, and I wrapped the stretched telephone cord around my finger. "Because Prudence slept with Henry?" Whatever they'd done together wasn't sleeping.

"Well...yes."

"Water under the bridge. Connie, listen, I need to let you go. I have to get to the hospital."

"That's right. Your mother. How is she?"

"On the mend."

"So terrible what happened. Everyone's talking about it. Please give her my regards."

"I will, thank you." If there was an arrest warrant for Prudence, Mother was yesterday's news.

We hung up, and I turned to Mr. Coffee.

More?

Tempting, but three cups in less than ten minutes was a lot, even for me. I nodded at my empty mug on the counter. "Later. Where is everyone?"

Grace went to swim practice. Anarchy went to work. Aggie went to the market. Max is outside. I haven't seen McCallester or your sister. He offered a sunny smile.

"Ellison?" Marjorie's voice carried.

"Kitchen."

She stumbled in, dodged a stack of boxes, and poured herself coffee.

"Good morning."

She grunted at me.

Max scratched at the backdoor, and I weaved through a forest of boxes and let him in.

He stared at me with liquid eyes until I gave him a treat.

"What's the plan?" Marjorie croaked.

"We can drive to the hospital together," I suggested. "Then I'll take Lloyd to the airport. When I get back, you can have the car, and I'll stay with Mother.

"What are you doing about the furniture and boxes?"

"Libba."

She snorted. "Good luck with that."

"Libba will come through." I hid my crossed fingers behind my back.

"When do we leave?"

I glanced at the clock. "Nine."

She refilled her mug. "I'll be ready."

I left her in the kitchen.

Marjorie was waiting when I returned thirty minutes later. She clutched a coffee mug and assessed my outfit. "Fancy."

I wore a silk wrap dress and pearls. "Lloyd Foster wants to show my work at his gallery in London. I can't wear shorts."

Marjorie wore a navy wrap skirt embroidered with Kelly green four-leaf clovers, wedge espadrilles, and a white cotton blouse. Mother would approve—especially since my sister had a tendency to wear low cut tops and short skirts. "I don't know. Your legs are still good. Maybe you should wear shorts."

"Ha, ha. Are you ready?" I opened the back door for Max and shooed him into the yard. Having him dig up my annuals was preferable to the damage he and McCallester might wreak if I left him in the house.

"Where's the cat?"

"Hiding." Still. And so well that Anarchy and I had failed to transfer him to Peters. We stepped outside, and I locked the door behind us.

The morning was lovely, but the humid air promised another scorching afternoon.

"After you drop your dealer friend at the airport, call the hospital. Mother will have a laundry list of things she wants."

"No problem." We settled into the car, and I inserted the ignition key.

Marjorie fiddled with the radio. "You listen to Q104?

"I like it." I kept my voice mild.

She sniffed. "I figured you'd listen to classical."

"Then you figured wrong." I did listen to classical, but we weren't exclusive. And I didn't want to argue with Marjorie about my love for contemporary music. "Connie Jackson called this morning."

"Who?"

"Connie Jackson. You knew her sister, Polly Mayer." I stopped at a sign and glanced at Marjorie, who wore a blank expression, as if I were discussing people she'd never met.

I swallowed my annoyance and turned onto Wornall Road. "Connie Jackson doesn't matter. It's what she told me. The police are looking for Prudence."

"Why?"

I'd been so flabbergasted by news of the arrest warrant, I hadn't asked. "I'm not sure."

"Because it might be for killing her mother, not hitting ours."

"I'm aware."

"Also, are you sure there's a warrant? Did someone see it?"

"Not that Connie mentioned."

"I hear she hates you."

"Connie?"

"Prudence." Marjorie had that right.

I braked for a red light.

"What did you do?" she asked.

"I stayed married to Henry."

"Henry swizzled that?"

"Swizzled?"

"It gets the point across. What was he thinking?" She sounded gobsmacked. "Prudence Davies? The woman with long teeth and gruesome smile?"

"That's her."

"He must have wanted to make you bleed."

"What do you mean?"

"If he took up with a gorgeous woman, you'd be furious. But Prudence? That had to hit your pride."

It had. "Henry was not discerning. He'd swivel anyone with female parts."

Marjorie winced. "I'm sorry."

"Sorry? For what?"

She reached over the gear shift and patted my arm. "I wasn't here for you."

Over the years, Marjorie and I had our ups and downs. Strike that. We'd had our tolerate-each-others and our downs. Never—not one time I could remember—had she expressed a wish to be there for me. I didn't trust the sentiment now. "I got by."

"And you're happy now." A statement, not a question.

"I am." I turned right at a traffic light.

"Not everyone gets a second chance." She opened the handbag on her lap, took out a lipstick, and lowered the visor. Using the mirror, she applied scarlet to her lips. "You're lucky."

"Is everything okay with you and Greg?"

"Okay is a good way to describe it." She glanced my way. "Don't worry. I won't be landing on your doorstep again." The last time she'd left her husband, she'd descended on me (less welcome than a plague of locusts). "We love each other. And we love the kids. We're comfortable."

"There are worse things."

"Seeing the sparks between you and Anarchy reminds me of what I'm missing."

"Anarchy and I have been married for less than a month. Of course there are still sparks. But marriage isn't sparks. It's a banked fire that promises to keep you warm the whole of your life." At least that's what I hoped. "You have that with Greg."

"I do," she ceded. "But sometimes I want excitement."

"Visit me more often."

I dropped Lloyd at the airport where he kissed my cheek, assured me he'd dine out on the story of his tumble down my stairs, and promised a telephone call about the show in London.

I hugged, apologized and thanked him then watched him pass through his gate. When he disappeared into the accordion thing that attached the plane to the airport, I found a payphone and called the hospital.

"Hello," said Marjorie.

"It's me. What does she need?"

"Nothing right now." We both knew that meant Mother would produce a mile-long list when running errands was less convenient.

"I'm on my way."

"Thank God."

"I take it she's in a sunny mood?"

"You're a regular George Carlin."

I could think of seven dirty words to describe the past few days. "I'm on my way."

"Thank God."

When Kansas City outgrew its downtown airport, the city leaders built the new facility in the Northland. For those of us who lived south of the river (the majority of the city's population) the drive seemed endless. If a councilman or the mayor had asked me, I'd have pointed them south. They hadn't asked, so I drove confusing highways to get back to the city as I understood it.

When I dug a quarter from my handbag, tossed it into a metal net, and crossed the Broadway bridge, I exhaled. I'd been known to miss the exit. Once I found myself in Liberty which was farther north than the airport. I still didn't know how I'd accomplished that.

On familiar streets, I let my mind wander. Was there really an arrest warrant for Prudence? An officer at her door might mean the police wanted her for questioning.

I imagined Prudence holding a pillow over her mother's face and ramming my mother into a busy intersection. Could she kill? My hands gripped the wheel and the answer seemed simple. Yes.

But had she?

I parked the car before reaching a satisfactory answer.

The hospital's corridors were crowded, and I nodded to people I knew.

"Ellison?"

I turned. "Good morning, Mrs. Murrow."

"Please. Call me Patience. How is your mother?"

"I'm on my way to see her."

Patience smoothed the fabric of her volunteer smock over her hips. She looked left and right as if checking for eavesdroppers. "Might I have a word?"

"Of course." I was in no hurry to get to Mother's hospital room. Although, where Patience expected us to hold a private conversation was beyond me.

"This way." She led me toward the hospital's entrance and took a right.

I followed her into the empty chapel.

"Is it true?" Her hand gripped the back of a pew.

"Is what true?" I had a suspicion. She wanted to know if there was a warrant for Prudence.

"Has my niece disappeared?"

"Disappeared?" My voice was too loud for a sanctuary, and we both winced.

"You didn't know?"

"I did not."

She sighed and sank into the closest pew. Then she buried her head in her hands. "I'm so sorry."

"For what?"

"For what Prudence did to your mother."

"You're sure?"

"Who else? Her claiming that Muriel's car was stolen is too convenient." Her head seemed to sink further into her hands. "I told my brother not to marry that woman." Patience was a pretty woman with a warm smile and kind eyes. Her condemnation of her niece was chilling. And convincing.

"If Prudence did hit Mother, it's not your fault."

Her shoulders shook. Unsure of what to say, I sat on the pew next to her.

This situation was beyond awkward. I patted her shoulder. "Mother will be fine."

Her breath caught.

"You're not responsible for Prudence or her actions."

She gave a tiny shake of her head. "Muriel couldn't have been an easy mother, but adults don't blame their parents for their problems. They accept responsibility for their actions."

"You believe that?" I asked.

"I do."

"Then, if Prudence did rear-end Mother, she bears full responsibility. You don't have anything to apologize for."

"Prudence is not an adult. She blames her mother for her mean streak and my brother for her need of male approval." She clasped her hands. "He wasn't around much when she was a little girl. He was building a company. He had to work."

I searched for something—anything—to say. But my mind was as blank as a fresh canvas. "Maybe Prudence is innocent."

Patience stiffened.

"Perhaps the car really was stolen. And she hasn't disappeared. She's just...not here."

"The police told her not to leave."

"Oh."

"She killed Muriel and tried to kill Francis."

"What about the other beneficiary in Muriel's will?"

Patience regarded me with wet, no longer kind eyes. "The family does not discuss that."

"I didn't mean to broach an uncomfortable subject. I apologize." Had Anarchy or Peters tracked down the heir?

"Do you know why people study history?"

The sudden shift in conversation left me near mute. "No."

"Those who fail to study history are doomed to repeat it. But studying history doesn't work." She pressed the pads of her fingers against her closed eyes. "The same mistakes are made. Over and over and over again." She dropped her hands and gazed at me as if she expected me to understand.

Since I didn't have the slightest idea what she meant, I offered a rueful smile and made a silent note to ask Anarchy about the missing beneficiary at the first opportunity.

Patience's expression turned brittle, and she stood. "I've kept you from your mother."

And I wasn't complaining.

When I rose from the pew, she said "Frances is lucky to have you."

I wasn't sure she'd agree. "Thank you."

Together, we returned to the hospital's busy entry where people pushed through the revolving doors in a steady stream.

"Is that Shirley Davidson?" I nodded toward a woman who'd covered her head with a Hermès scarf and perched dark glasses on her nose.

Patience narrowed her eyes. "I believe so."

"I need to speak with her." Mother wanted to reschedule dinner. "Would you please excuse me?"

"Of course."

I hesitated. "Patience, no one blames you for what happened to Mother."

"Thank you, Ellison. Give Frances my best." She left me.

"Shirley," I called.

The woman in the scarf kept walking.

"Mrs. Billings!"

Her step hitched, but she kept moving away.

I followed. But not fast enough. The woman stepped into the elevator and jabbed at a button.

I stared as the doors closed. The dark glasses. The pinched lips. The glint of the enormous emerald on her right hand as she clutched her scarf beneath her chin.

I sighed with annoyance. I just needed thirty seconds of her time. Why had she pretended not to know me? The last thing I needed was another mystery.

CHAPTER TWELVE

I returned home late in the afternoon and paused on the front stoop. The furniture. The boxes. The cat and dog determined to destroy everything we owned. After a day spent with Mother, I was too spent to handle even the smallest problem.

Maybe a glass of wine on the patio, far from the chaos? That was exactly the ticket. I conjured soft music, golden light, and a gentle breeze. With the image of chilled wine and a shaded chaise front and center in my mind, I cracked open the front door.

My jaw dropped. The foyer was empty. Well, empty of Anarchy's furniture. My belongings—the bombé chest, the art, the oriental were all where they belonged.

I slipped inside and peeked into the living room. Everything was in place.

It was as if an organization fairy had banished chaos. That, or Libba had worked a miracle.

"You're home." Aggie, who'd paired a lavender and lime caftan with purple hoop earrings, joined me in the living room.

I blinked at her ensemble, then turned a slow circle. "Where did it go?"

"Next door."

The effort required to move so much boggled the mind. "How?"

Aggie flashed me a grin. "She arrived with a small army."

"They took everything?"

"Not the boxes."

"Oh." Disappointment dragged on my shoulders. So many boxes. "Where are they?"

"In the study." Aggie shook her head. "It was a busy afternoon. I'm afraid there's no dinner."

"No problem. We'll go to the club." I completed another stunned-but-happy circle. "I need to send Libba flowers. Or a bottle of gin. A case of gin."

"I didn't think she had it in her, but she was like a brigadier general, issuing orders, directing troops. And I believe she's got everything arranged at Dr. Ardmore's house."

The furniture was gone. That was one huge problem solved. "Have we found McCallester?"

"Not yet. But Max is over his gas."

More good news. A wave of optimism lifted me, and I rode its crest into the kitchen.

Like the foyer and the living room, the kitchen was back to normal. No boxes, and Mr. Coffee maintained his pride of place spot on the counter. He even gave me a saucy wink.

"How's your mother?" Aggie had followed me.

Max scratched at the back door, and I let him in and gave him a treat. "She wants to go home."

"So she's feeling better?"

"Yes, but the hospital's not ready to discharge her. She's being difficult."

Aggie refrained from stating the obvious—*difficult* was Mother's middle name. "How's your father holding up?"

"He's fine. Marjorie spent the afternoon helping him reconfigure the family room into a bedroom. According to the doctor, Mother should avoid stairs." She'd pooh-poohed the suggestion till Daddy reminded her she had both a broken leg and arm. He couldn't carry her like a bride. "I can't believe it's all cleaned up. How full is the study?"

"You won't be using the phone in there. Reaching the desk is impossible, but at least the rest of the house is clear."

"Even the family room?" It had been packed to the gills.

Aggie nodded.

"You must have worked all afternoon.

"Libba had her troops carry the boxes."

"I'll go next door and thank her."

I stepped outside and cut across the lawn to the gate that separated my yard from Charlie's. The gate stood open so our dogs could visit.

Pansy greeted me with a pink-tongued smile.

When I reached the patio, I rubbed behind her ears. "How are you, pretty girl?"

Her grin widened.

I knocked, and Libba opened the door. She wore one of Charlie's button-downs. The shirt was wrinkled, and streaks of grime marred the rolled-up sleeves and front. She'd tied a flowered cotton scarf over her head. If she'd started the day with make-up, the blush and lipstick had long since worn off. Glamorous Libba looked like ten miles of bad road.

"You're amazing," I told her.

She gave me a tired smile. "Keep talking."

"A veritable sorceress. Like Glinda the Good. But better."

"I'm listening."

"A worker of miracles."

She nodded and stepped away from the door. "Do you want a martini?"

"An angel of mercy."

"Come in. There's a pitcher on the counter."

As advertised, a crystal pitcher waited on the counter. A shaft of sunlight hit it, and the contents sparkled brighter than a promise.

Libba opened a cabinet. "Here's a glass."

"Where's Charlie?"

"Not home yet."

"You're drinking alone?"

"Don't judge. I worked my butt off. And I'm not drinking alone. You're with me."

In the face of her unassailable logic, I accepted the filled-to-the-rim glass and sipped. "Delicious."

"Of course. I made it. Let me show you the house." She led me into the front hall. "Living room first."

Where there was once a sad recliner, now sat wingback chairs, a library table, and a Chippendale butler's tray filled with a variety of liquor bottles. All positioned on a palace-sized oriental rug.

"We need a couch. Celeste sent you lots of chairs and tables and chests and even bookcases. No couches."

Thank heavens. The couches wouldn't have fit in my house. "The room looks fabulous." I stepped inside and let my fingers trace the inlay on a set of nesting tables. "I hope Charlie likes it."

Libba's smile looked fixed.

"You did tell him?"

"Tell him what?"

"That you were taking the furniture."

She waved her manicured fingers. "He'll be thrilled."

"Libba."

"Trust me." She grabbed my free hand. "Come see the dining room."

Eight burr walnut dining chairs covered in buttery soft claret-hued leather surrounded an art-deco table. A large box stood in the corner. "A chandelier?" I asked.

"If you don't want it, I'll have an electrician install it tomorrow."

I looked up at the brass monstrosity hanging above the table. "I don't want it."

"The bedrooms are furnished. We just need mattresses. I can't thank you enough."

"Thank Anarchy. And it's me who should be thanking you."

"You already did."

"We're going to the club for dinner. Would you and Charlie like to join us?"

"Not tonight. It's all I can do to put one foot in front of the other. Besides, when you take us to dinner, I want the Bristol or the Peppercorn Duck Club."

"Done."

"How's Frances?"

"As you'd expect." I drank. Deeply.

"Let's sit. My back is killing me." She led me to the living room and sank onto the nearest wingback.

I chose a club chair. "You heard about Prudence?"

"She's missing. Highly suspicious."

How did Libba, who'd spent her day moving furniture, hear about Prudence? Who stole my thunder? I asked as much.

She gave a tired shrug. "Jinx called."

My brows lifted. "Jinx calls you here?"

"What?" She sounded defensive.

"Jinx calls you at his house. You spend most nights here."

"How do you know?"

"Your car is in the drive."

"Aren't you the nosy neighbor?"

"Nope. That's Marian. I'm just observant. So, when's the wedding?"

"Ellison!"

"I'm happy for you. Charlie is a good guy."

"He is." Her lids closed, and a dreamy smile curled her lips.

"Doesn't mean I'm getting married. Let's talk about something else."

"Where do you think Prudence went?"

She rolled her shoulders. "No idea. Don't care. I have enough on my plate already." As hints went, Libba's wasn't subtle. She meant I had plenty on my plate. Leave the police investigation alone.

I looked into my glass. How was it empty already? Then I glanced at my watch. "I should get home. You're sure you won't come to dinner?"

"Positive." She stretched her legs and leaned her head against the chair's back.

I stood. "I'll see myself out."

She gave a half-hearted wave. "Have a nice dinner."

"May I bring you something?"

"Nope. I intend to finish my drink, shower, and fall into bed. Charlie can take a self-guided tour."

I hoped he liked what he saw.

Anarchy drove. If he was nervous about his first dinner at the club as a member, he didn't show it. His left hand sat at twelve o'clock on the steering wheel. His right hand held mine.

"Ellison, do you still swim in the morning?"

I swiveled and looked at my sister in the backseat. "In theory. I haven't been good about going since we got home from Italy."

Grace, who was less than thrilled to spend a weekend night at the club with her mother, stepfather and aunt, snorted.

"Can we swim tomorrow?" asked Marjorie.

"When I go, I usually leave the house before six. Is that a problem?"

Marjorie pursed her lips, and I was sure she'd tell me to forget the idea. "I need the exercise."

"Then tomorrow, we swim." There were Italian calories still waiting to be burned.

Anarchy parked. We walked through the club's entrance and spotted Laine Jackson.

"See," I told Grace. "You're not the only teenager forced into a family dinner."

Grace rolled her eyes and walked toward her friend.

No sooner had Grace approached than the girls were surrounded by older ladies. Laine's paternal grandmother, Elaine Jackson, Patience Murrow, Sally Billings (which surprised me), and Susan Matthews.

"Interesting," I murmured.

"What?" asked Anarchy.

"Patience disliked Muriel, and Sally was Muriel's best friend" Now that I looked. Neither Patience nor Sally looked pleased to be in the grouping.

"So they can't be friends?"

I studied his face. Was he teasing? His steady gaze said no. "Believe me." I nodded toward the women. "They're not friends."

"Ellison," Elaine Jackson called.

"Oh dear Lord." I forced a polite expression and approached the group. "Elaine, how nice to see you. Patience, Sally. Susan." I offered each woman a smile. "Laine."

"We were just chatting with your daughter. She's lovely." Grace wore a Lilly shift and summer sandals that were still white, not the dingy gray they'd achieve later in the season. Her hair was pulled back in a sleek ponytail. And a pleasant smile touched her lips.

"Thank you, Elaine. I believe we'll keep her."

"How's Frances?"

"On the mend. She wants to go home."

"Of course she does. Give her my regards." Elaine was one of those women who'd met adversity and wrestled it to its knees. Now she believed herself immune to fortune's foibles.

I knew better. No one was immune. Still, I envied her certainty that she could weather any storm. "I'll do that. How's Connie? I saw her at the hospital."

"So much drama." Elaine shook her head as if Connie were a heavy cross to bear.

Laine's young face tightened. "She broke her collarbone."

"She's clumsy, dear. I warned Parker…" Infinite criticism lived in what Elaine left unsaid. She didn't approve of her daughter-in-law and only held her tongue for her granddaughter's sake.

I was lucky. Henry's mother never criticized me (as far as I knew), and Celeste lived half a country away. Poor Connie had to deal with Elaine. Regularly.

Susan stepped into the awkward silence. "Grace was just telling us you've resumed swimming in the mornings."

"Yes." Starting tomorrow.

Elaine pressed her palms to her sizable bosom. "If it were me, I might never go in the water again." She was referring to me swimming into a body in a dark pool.

I smiled brightly. "I've swum at dawn for years. Hundreds of times. Maybe thousands. I've only had one problem."

"But what a problem."

My smile faltered.

"Ellison is right," said Susan. "A woman can't let one bad experience keep her from the things she enjoys."

Anarchy waved at us. I waved back. And the women's gazes shifted to my new husband.

"I forgot," said Elaine. "You're a newlywed." Her eyes narrowed. "Is that Marjorie?"

"It is."

"Here to see your mother."

"Yes, ma'am."

"She lives in Ohio."

"That's right."

"Well, enjoy your dinner." Grace and I were dismissed.

"Thank you," I replied. We beat a hasty retreat.

"Their husbands are playing golf then meeting them for dinner," Grace told me.

"And Laine?"

"She drove the ladies here. Her grandmother insisted she stay."

"See," I said. "Your night could be worse. Also, we're all exhausted, and Marjorie wants to get up early. You'll be home by eight."

We joined Anarchy and Marjorie at a table near the windows overlooking the golf course.

Marjorie lifted a water glass to her lips. "Anarchy was just telling me Prudence has disappeared."

"Is there a warrant for her arrest, or did you want her for questioning?" The question had niggled at me all day.

Before Anarchy could answer, a waiter arrived and served drinks. Scotch for Anarchy and Marjorie, a martini for me, and a Tab with two limes for Grace.

Anarchy raised his glass. "To Libba."

We clinked glasses, and I studied my husband. He was avoiding my question. And I wondered why.

"Can we not talk about Prudence or car accidents or Mother's injuries, just for an hour or two?" Marjorie sipped her scotch and sighed. "Grace, tell us about the kids you're babysitting."

"Ruby and Barr. She's five. He's six. They're adorable."

"Ruby?" Disapproval dripped from Marjorie's tone, heavy as the marble-size pearls around her neck.

"Grace didn't name the child."

"I should think not."

"You sound like Mother."

"There's no reason to be mean."

Anarchy chuckled.

We ordered. Hamburgers for Grace and Anarchy. Salads with dressing on the side for Marjorie and me.

Friends stopped by the table, asked after Mother, and offered their best wishes for her speedy recovery.

At one point, Grace leaned close to me and whispered, "People are staring."

"Let them," I whispered back.

We were home shortly after eight.

"I'm going to Peggy's." Grace disappeared out the back door.

"I'm going to bed." Marjorie disappeared up the back stairs.

"We're going to sit on the patio and enjoy a nightcap." Anarchy grabbed my hand and led me outside.

We cuddled together on a wrought iron love seat and gazed at the velvet sky.

"So." I took his hand in mine. "Is there an arrest warrant for Prudence?"

"Yes."

"But she's missing."

"How did you hear?" Anarchy draped his free arm over my shoulders.

"Her aunt told me."

"Any idea where she'd go?"

"Nope." Prudence and I weren't friends. I didn't know her secrets. "What did Peters find?"

"When?"

"In Muriel's Mark III."

Anarchy stiffened. "This stays between us."

"Okay."

"A bottle of chloroform."

I thought for a long moment. "It would be easier to suffocate someone if they were knocked out."

"Exactly."

"I thought Muriel fought her attacker."

"Chloroform's not an exact science. What do your friends think? Is Prudence guilty."

"Yes."

"And you? Do you agree?"

I considered my answer. "I'm not so sure. Tell me about the heir."

"A woman named Lillith Ames. There was an address listed in the will, but she no longer lives there."

"Who is she? Why did Muriel include her?"

"Mrs. Jarret left Miss Ames a million dollars. And we have no idea why."

A million dollars? Wow. Muriel was better off than I'd imagined. "How much did Prudence get?"

"The rest." He took in my curious expression and added, "Close to five million. Plus the houses."

"Houses?"

"There's a lake house." He rubbed the back of her neck. "We checked. Prudence isn't there."

"Did she ever offer an alibi? Before she disappeared, I mean."

"Nothing we could corroborate."

"But you didn't arrest her."

"No. Something felt...off."

We both stared into the gathering darkness.

"Enough talk about murder." Anarchy's fingers brushed my shoulder. "How did you end things with Lloyd?"

"We're traveling to London next summer."

Anarchy's eyes glinted in the golden light spilling from the kitchen windows. "I'm proud of you."

Words my first husband never uttered. My heart swelled. "I love you."

Anarchy stood and pulled me to my feet.

"Where are we going?"

"Inside."

"What about the nightcap."

"Forget about the nightcap." He kissed me.

"What nightcap?"

I yawned and tapped on Marjorie's door. "Are you up?"

A beast on the other side growled at me.

"Still not a morning person."

Now the beast grunted. "Coffee."

"Mr. Coffee's working on it as we speak."

Marjorie replied with silence, and I turned my back on her door.

"Wait!"

I glanced over my shoulder. "What?"

"Do you have a suit I can borrow?"

"Of course." We were roughly the same size. "I'll bring you one."

Two minutes later, I delivered a one-piece suit to a remarkably ungrateful houseguest. Then I descended to the kitchen where Mr. Coffee gave me a sunny smile.

I poured myself a cup, filled a thermos, and took a travel mug from the cabinet for Marjorie. Then I waited. Minutes ticked by. I debated going upstairs and prodding, but I valued my life.

When Marjorie emerged from the back stairway, she grunted at me. "Do you have towels?"

I nodded toward the folded beach towels waiting on the counter and handed her a to-go coffee.

"What are we waiting for?"

Her. "Nothing."

We collected the towels and walked toward the front door.

"Do you have goggles?" she asked.

"Upstairs."

"I need goggles."

"Fine." I handed her my towel, the post-swim thermos, and the car keys. "I'll run upstairs and fetch a pair. Meet you outside."

She grunted. Cavemen grunted less than my sister in the early morning.

I jogged up the stairs and hurried toward our bedroom. At the rate we were going, we'd be doing laps with the swim team.

Bang!

I froze. I'd heard too many gunshots not to recognize one.

Anarchy burst through the bedroom door. His hands closed around my upper arms, and his eyes searched my face. "Ellison! You're okay."

"Fine. I'm fine—oh, no." I pulled free of Anarchy's hold, ran down the stairs, and threw open the front door.

Marjorie lay on the driveway in a growing pool of blood.

Anarchy, who'd followed me, ran to her. "Stay inside. Call for an ambulance and the police. Now."

I raced to the kitchen, ignored Mr. Coffee's questioning brow, grabbed the receiver, and dialed. "Operator, we need an ambulance. Someone shot my sister."

CHAPTER THIRTEEN

I rode to the hospital in the ambulance with Marjorie. Anarchy, who'd secured my promise that I'd go nowhere alone, stayed at the house to process the crime scene. My—our—home was a crime scene. Again.

I'd waved goodbye to my husband, whose eyes narrowed with anger, my daughter, whose eyes widened with shock, and a dog who was ready to search the neighborhood for the perpetrator. Or squirrels. He'd be happy to search for squirrels.

"Ellison?" Marjorie's voice was barely a croak.

I leaned forward and peeked around the EMT who monitored her vitals. "I'm here."

"She shot me."

She? My stomach clenched. "Who?"

"A woman. She called your name. She was behind a bush in the witch's yard." She meant my next-door neighbor, Margaret Hamilton, who I'd once accused of riding a broomstick at midnight.

"Margaret's not so bad."

"She shot me."

"Margaret?"

"No." A tear trickled down Marjorie's cheek. "Is it supposed to hurt this much?"

"You'll be fine," said the EMT. "I've seen plenty of gunshot wounds. This one's not bad. The bullet passed clean through your arm."

Another tear joined the first.

"I'll give you something for the pain." "He pulled out a needle, and I closed my eyes.

"Still hurts." Her gaze found mine. "She shot me."

"In the arm." There were much worse places to be shot.

"You don't sound sympathetic." And Marjorie didn't sound like herself. Typical Marjorie was drama and wailing and Chicken Little running about. Now she sounded sleepy.

"I am sympathetic." And angry. And, since she mentioned the woman called my name and the bullet was meant for me, I felt guilty. "And I'm sorry."

"Why are you sorry? You didn't shoot me."

"You just said the bullet was meant for me."

"I never liked Prudence Jarret."

"Davies," I corrected. "Prudence shot you?" If Prudence had done this, I'd wring her scrawny neck and knock her horse teeth down her throat. Not really. But imagining getting even made the guilt bearable.

She pursed her lips. "Who else?"

I had no idea.

"Mother will have kittens." Marjorie giggled. Giggled. Either the pain meds had kicked in or… "Did you hit your head when you fell?"

"No. Why?"

"Because nothing about telling Mother is funny." I rubbed my hands across my face. "Maybe we don't tell her."

"Oh, please. The woman who lives across the street from you, Gladys, has already called."

Who was Gladys? "The hospital turns off incoming calls at night."

"It's morning."

And what a morning it promised to be.

The ambulance slowed to a stop, and the attendants slid Marjorie's gurney from the vehicle.

"Call Greg." She used a sing-song voice.

"Okay."

"Now."

"Okay."

"Tell him the bullet was meant for you."

I sighed. "Okay."

"Do it now, Ellison."

I watched as they wheeled her into the ER, then I trudged to the payphones and realized I didn't have my purse.

I dialed the operator and asked to place a collect call.

Rather than face the phone, I twisted so I could watch the room. Someone had called my name then shot my sister. It didn't take a genius to conclude they'd shot the wrong woman. I needed to be careful, to watch my back.

The number of people in the ER was sparse, but they all stared at me. Hardly surprising. I wore a swimsuit and a sheer cover up that stopped six inches above my knees. They all had the benefit of clothes.

The operator rang Marjorie's number, and Greg answered on the third ring.

"Collect call from Ellison Jones. Will you accept the charges?"

"Yes." He sounded sleepy.

The operator hung up, and Greg asked, "Is your mother okay?"

"On the mend. I'm calling about Marjorie."

"Marjorie? What's wrong with Marjorie?" No sleep in his voice now.

"It's a minor wound, but she's been shot."

"Shot?" His voice boomed through the telephone line, and I held the receiver away from my ear. "How?" he demanded. "Why? Where?"

"In front of the house." I took a deep breath and tightened my grip on the receiver. "Someone mistook her for me."

His silence was deafening.

"She was shot in the arm. The bullet went clean through. She'll be fine," I assured him. "We're at the hospital."

"Where's Anarchy?"

"Processing the scene."

"Who shot her?"

"I'm not sure, but I've never seen Anarchy so angry." Angry wasn't the right word. Anarchy had burned with a cold fire. His rage was frightening. "He'll find the shooter."

"What does Frances say?"

"She doesn't know yet."

He gave a bitter chuckle. "I don't envy you that conversation."

"I'd rather be shot." It was nothing less than the truth. Just the thought of telling Mother made my blood crystallize.

"Where's Marjorie now?"

"With the doctor. She'll call you as soon as she can."

"Should I come to Kansas City?"

Did Marjorie want him here? The ins and outs of their marriage mystified me. No way was I taking responsibility for bringing Greg to Kansas City. "Ask Marjorie when you talk to her."

A nurse approached me. "Mrs. Jones?"

She was vaguely familiar.

I read her name tag. "Is my sister okay, Pam?"

"Yes. But your husband called." Her face flushed. "He says you're to stay in the ER with your sister. That, or we're to arrange an escort for you to your mother's room."

Mother? Before seven? No, thank you. "Greg, I'll have Marjorie call you.

"Let me know if there's any change."

"Promise." I hung up the phone and followed the nurse to the treatment room.

She jerked back the curtain, and I stared at my sister. Her color was good (probably due to her deep tan) and her eyes were closed.

"She's out cold." Pam nodded toward Marjorie's bandaged arm. "There'll be no lasting damage."

"Will it scar?"

"A bullet passed through her arm."

"So that's a yes?"

Pam nodded. Who knew nods could be sarcastic?

"Do you have a plastic surgeon on call?"

"For an arm?"

"Please?"

Pam's lips pinched together.

"Whoever shot her mistook her for me." I pointed at my sleeping sister. "She'll hold that scar against me for the rest of our lives. A cold-shoulder on Christmas. A brush off at birthdays. Ice cold slights on our parents' anniversary."

"I'll see what I can do." Pam paused at the entrance to the room and gave me a look perfected by mothers of unruly toddlers. "Stay here."

I waited. I twiddled my thumbs. I hoped. I hatched revenge plots.

When a doctor pulled back the curtain, I blurted, "You're the plastic surgeon?"

"I'm Dr. Clay." He removed Marjorie's bandages and studied the stitches. He pursed his lips. He nodded.

"Thank you for coming."

"You're welcome." He shifted his gaze to me. "The ER doc did a fine job. Scarring will be minimal."

"So there will be scarring?"

"A bullet tore through her skin."

Marjorie stirred and moaned softly.

"There's nothing you can do?" Desperation colored my tone.

"I'm sorry." He left us, and I sat in the uncomfortable chair and thought. Hard.

Marjorie would be livid. I cringed in anticipation. I hadn't pulled the trigger, but I would get the blame. Why would Prudence shoot at me? She'd come to my house and asked for my help. I could hardly take her side if I was dead. Also, why shoot me now? Prudence had better motive to kill me when she was swizzling my husband. Back when my death might mean she became the next Mrs. Henry Russell.

Nothing made sense.

"Ellison?" Marjorie's voice was barely a whisper.

I clasped her hand. "I'm here."

"Did you talk to Greg?"

"I did. He wants you to phone him when you're up to it."

"When can I go home?"

"I don't know. Let's ask." I pushed the call button.

A moment later, someone drew back the curtain. I turned to ask the nurse about discharge, but Anarchy stood in the room's entrance. His lean face was made up of unforgiving planes, and his eyes were hard as diamonds. "Marjorie, how are you?"

"My arm hurts."

He winced. "I bet. Ellison, a word?"

"Of course." I stood and followed him into the hallway.

He wrapped me in a tight hug. "How are you?"

With my cheek pressed against his chest, I breathed him in. "I'm fine."

"Did Marjorie see who shot her?"

"I can hear you," Marjorie called.

And I didn't want to accuse Prudence. "You should get the story from the horse's mouth."

"Who are you calling a horse?"

He loosened his hold, and we gazed into each other's eyes. My gaze said she's on pain meds. His gaze said he wouldn't rest till he caught the shooter.

"Prudence Davies shot me."

Anarchy stiffened, and he strode into Marjorie's exam room. "You're sure?"

"Who else?"

I didn't have an answer for that, but Marjorie's certainty felt wrong. I followed him into the room. "If Prudence wanted me dead, she'd stab me in the back."

Marjorie rolled her eyes.

"Wait." I held up a finger. "How did Prudence know I'd be outside before six?" It stretched credulity to imagine she'd simply sat outside my house in the hope I'd emerge before the sun.

"Who knew your plans for this morning?" asked Anarchy.

"The ladies we saw at the club last night."

"Who else?"

"Whoever they told." I shrugged. "Although it's not exactly hot gossip."

"Prudence's aunt was in the group," said Marjorie.

"Yes. But I doubt Patience told Prudence. I doubt Patience speaks to Prudence."

When we got home, a strange car was parked in the drive.

"Who's here?" Marjorie cradled her bandaged arm against her chest.

I eyed the silver Mercedes sedan. "No idea."

Anarchy stiffened. "They're waiting inside."

"Aggie wouldn't let just anyone in."

We stood in the drive and stared at the house.

"Your neighbor is watching," said Marjorie.

"Marian's always watching."

She's like Gladys Kravitz."

"Who?"

"The nosy neighbor from Bewitched." Marjorie side-eyed me. "But you're no Samantha Stephens."

"If I was, I'd know who was inside."

Anarchy strode toward the door.

"He's not happy," Marjorie observed. "Have you seen him angry before?"

"Not like this."

We followed him into the house, and I peeked into the living room. Sally Billings sat on a loveseat. Her hair was a fluffy white helmet, and shell pink lipstick colored her mouth. She wore a navy St. John suit and sensible pumps. She also wore gold earrings, a gold watch, and a gold ring on her left hand set with a diamond the size of Maryland. She saw me and offered a tentative smile.

"Mrs. Billings?" I made her name a question.

"Your housekeeper let me in." Her gaze darted from me to Anarchy to Marjorie's bandaged arm. "May we speak in private?"

"I need to change." I still wore my swimsuit, a cover up, and flip-flops. "Then I need to get back to the hospital."

"This won't take long." Her eyes pleaded.

"Of course," I ceded. "Would you like coffee?"

"Your housekeeper already offered."

"Anarchy." I looked into my husband's eyes. "Would you ask Aggie to bring us coffee?" Sally might not want any, but I did.

He held my gaze for long seconds before giving a curt nod and disappearing down the hall.

"I believe I'll go upstairs and rest," Marjorie announced.

When she'd climbed the stairs, I turned to Sally. "What did you want to discuss?"

"Prudence."

"What about her?"

"She didn't kill her mother or rear-end yours or shoot your sister." Sally already knew someone shot Marjorie. Bad news traveled fast.

"Are you Prudence's alibi?"

Sally's cheeks flushed. "No. But I know her. She wouldn't do those things."

This was my chance. "Who's Lillith Ames?"

Sally looked down at her lap. "That's Muriel's secret."

"Lillith is the only other person with a financial motive."

"Lillith didn't kill Muriel."

"How can you be sure?"

"She's dead." As alibis went, it was a good one.

"Coffee?" Aggie stepped into the living room and put a tray on the coffee table. "I made muffins."

"Aggie is a marvelous cook. May we tempt you?"

"Just coffee, please," Sally replied.

I poured her a cup. "Cream or sugar?"

"Black."

I handed her the saucer, fixed myself a cup, and put a muffin on a plate. Then I gave Sally an expectant look. "You were saying..."

She waited till Aggie disappeared into the hallway, then leaned forward and whispered. "Lillith is dead."

"Who, exactly, is Lillith?"

An eternity passed, then Sally put her cup on the coffee table and resumed the study of her hands in her lap.

"Right now, Prudence is the only suspect." My voice was gentle.

She looked up, her eyes pleading. "All these years I've kept Muriel's secret." She closed her lids. "Lillith is Muriel's daughter."

My cup rattled in its saucer. "Muriel named her daughter after a demon?"

"Muriel named her daughter after a woman who refused to be subservient to Adam."

I swallowed. "My mistake."

"Muriel had an affair when she was a girl. She had a daughter."

I tried to imagine bitter, cane-wielding Muriel having an affair. "What happened to the baby's father?"

"Muriel's parents didn't find the young man suitable."

I sat in stunned silence. Muriel Jarret had an affair.

"She loved him," Sally said softly. Sadly.

"What happened?"

"Her parents didn't approve." Sally wrung her hands. "Muriel gave up both the man and the baby."

I'd never heard so much as a whisper of this scandal. "They must have worked very hard to keep the story quiet."

"I don't think anyone in Kansas City knew except Muriel, her parents, and me."

"No one told Prudence?"

"No."

"What about Muriel's husband? Did he know?"

Sally winced. "Palmer found out. Early on."

"She told him?"

"His virginal bride had stretch marks. Their marriage was never a good one."

"Did Muriel know Lillith was dead?"

She gave a tiny nod. "Yes."

"Then why include her in the will?"

"There's a per stirpes provision."

"Pardon?"

Sally's expression softened. "I remember the day Muriel told me she was a grandmother. The provision means Lillith's child will inherit her share."

Lillith's child had a motive for murder.

"I guess we should add the lawyer to the list of people who knew Muriel's secret."

"The lawyer?"

"The lawyer." She picked up her coffee cup and took a sip. "Hunter Tafft. He drafted Muriel's will."

CHAPTER FOURTEEN

I found Anarchy in the kitchen with Aggie. He leaned against the counter and lifted a did-it-go-okay brow. I offered him a small I'm-fine-and-I'm-not-thinking-about-Hunter-Tafft smile and shifted my gaze

Bread, bacon, sliced tomatoes, lettuce, a bowl of fruit salad, and carrot strips spread across the counter.

Aggie held up a slice of fresh bread which she'd bought from a baker, not the grocery store. "Are you hungry?"

"Starving." I hadn't wanted to eat a muffin when Sally declined.

"Do you want mayo?"

"Please."

"Lunch in five minutes."

"Perfect. I'll change." I flashed Anarchy another smile, then escaped upstairs and traded my swimsuit for linen pants and a tee-shirt. My face in the mirror looked pale, and I swiped blush across my cheeks. Mother had hoped—assiduously hoped—I'd fall in love with and marry Hunter. Now, less than a week back from my honeymoon, I wanted to call him. Yes, it was about

Lillith Ames and her child, but if Anarchy reached out to a woman from his past, I'd be hurt and jealous and angry. I took a calming breath. Anarchy hadn't been married to Henry. He didn't have my trust issues. He might not care if I called Hunter.

When I returned to the kitchen, Aggie was wiping down the already spotless counter. "Anarchy and your lunches are on the patio."

"Thank you." What would I do without Aggie?

"Iced tea?"

"Tab."

She nodded, and I stepped outside. Wrought iron furniture dotted the patio, and a large umbrella (sunny yellow with scalloped edges and white piping) shaded the table where Anarchy waited for me.

He rose when I approached. "What did Sally Billings say?"

"That Prudence is innocent." I took my seat and scratched behind Max's ear. He looked at me with soulful, liquid eyes. Would I please share my bacon? Pretty please? With sugar on top?

Anarchy raked a hand through his hair. "Prudence looks guilty."

"Yesterday, you weren't convinced."

"Yesterday, no one had shot at you."

I picked up a carrot stick. "There's another possibility."

"The other heir?" He shook his head. "Lillith Ames is dead."

He knew? And he hadn't said a word. "How long have you known?"

"I found out yesterday afternoon."

"And you didn't tell me?"

"It wasn't on the top of my list. Also, we've been busy."

I couldn't argue with that. "Lillith Ames had a child."

The back door opened before Anarchy replied, and Aggie stepped onto the patio carrying a glass of ice with two limes and a bright pink can.

"Thank you, Aggie." I nodded toward my plate. "This looks delicious."

Aggie gave me an indulgent smile. "You're welcome. Enjoy." Then she returned to the kitchen.

Max settled onto the patio bricks and stared at me with hope in his eyes.

"You were saying?" Anarchy asked.

"Sally said Lillith had a child."

"Did she give you a name?"

"No."

Anarchy winced. "She lived in Florida. Is that where she gave birth?"

"I don't know."

He put down his sandwich and scowled at the blue spruce at the back of our yard. "Unless we know where to look, it could take weeks to find him or her."

I took a large sip of Tab to erase the sudden dryness in my mouth. "There's someone who may know."

"Who?"

I took another sip. Some people complained about Tab's metallic taste, but I loved the stuff. And if I added enough lime, it barely tasted like nickel. We should buy more. I should tell Aggie. Also, we'd need more limes...

"Who, Ellison?"

I put down the glass. "Hunter Tafft."

"He's been avoiding our calls."

"I can get through to him." Once upon a time, Hunter gave me the secret code to get past the receptionist who screened his calls. "Not today. But when he's in the office."

"Then call him on Monday. We need to locate Lillith's heir."

The back door opened, and Jinx appeared. She paused, taking in Anarchy and me at the wrought-iron table, the yellow umbrella, Max waiting for bacon, the color of my geraniums, and the health of my hostas. "Sorry to interrupt..."

I didn't believe that for a second. "Would you care to join us?"

Anarchy stood and pulled out a chair for her.

"I've already eaten, but I'll sit for a few minutes." She sank into the chair. "What a gorgeous day. Hardly any humidity. How's Marjorie?"

"You heard?"

"Everyone's heard. Marian Dixon lit up the phone lines like a Christmas tree."

"She does that."

"Does Frances know?"

I winced. "Yes." It had not been a pleasant conversation. She'd stared at Marjorie's bandaged arm and her adult daughters clad in swimsuits, then sent us home to change. "I imagine she'll call shortly to ask why I'm not at the hospital."

Jinx shifted her gaze to Anarchy. "I heard Prudence is the shooter. Is that true?"

"We don't know who pulled the trigger."

Jinx eyed my plate. "May I?"

I nodded, and she helped herself to a carrot stick, which she pointed at my husband. "You have to admit, Prudence looks guilty. Also, I hear she's missing."

Anarchy ignored her searching gaze and took a bite of his sandwich.

I lifted my glass. "Maybe she's away with that man you told me about."

Jinx's forehead creased and her lips turned downward.

"What?" I asked.

"Faulty intelligence." Jinx was seldom wrong, and mistakes irked her. Right now, her brows drew together and her lips pursed.

"She's not seeing someone?"

"Oh, she's seeing someone. But he's married."

Anarchy rested his forearms on the table and leaned toward

my friend. "Jinx, how do you know these things? Do you have hotel clerks on your payroll?"

She rolled her eyes. "Don't be silly. Chambermaids have much better intel."

Was she serious?

Her Cheshire cat grin gave nothing away.

"Who is Prudence seeing now?" I asked.

Jinx shook her head. "Nope. I've been wrong once. I won't say a word till I know for certain." She bit into the carrot stick, then her gaze wandered toward Charlie's house. "I hear Libba's practically living at Charlie's."

"You'd have to ask her."

"I will." She munched her carrot.

"Have you heard anything about Shirley Davidson?" I asked.

"Shirley?"

"I saw her at the hospital wearing sunglasses inside. She pretended not to recognize me."

Her expression turned mournful. "I heard she might be ill."

"Ill?"

"Cancer."

My hands dropped to my lap. "Oh, no."

"It's still a secret." She clasped her hands together. "That poor woman already had plenty to deal with." She meant Sabra.

"What kind of cancer?"

"I don't know. Yet." She stood and stared at my husband. "You're sure Prudence didn't shoot Marjorie?"

"No comment."

"Ellison, you married a vault." There was grudging respect in her voice. "I'll see you at the party."

We watched her walk toward the house.

"That woman's talents are wasted. She could run the CIA." There was grudging respect in Anarchy's voice as well. "What party?"

"I forgot."

"Forgot what?"

I leaned my head against the back of the chair and stared at the underside of the umbrella. "Tonight. It's the club pool party."

"And we're going?"

I nodded. "If you don't want to, I can take Marjorie as my date."

"I wouldn't miss it."

"You may change your mind after attending one." Just thinking about it ruined my appetite. I ignored my sandwich, picked at the fruit salad, and nibbled on a carrot stick. When Anarchy finished his lunch, I slipped Max the uneaten bacon.

His stubby tail wagged his thanks.

When we returned to the kitchen, Aggie held out a stack of messages.

"I can't right now." I'd gladly put off till Tuesday phone calls I could make today.

She gave the stack a gentle shake. "You should look through them."

Aggie seldom insisted. Instead, she made fabulous meals, didn't scold me when I failed to eat them, kept the house running, listened almost as well as Mr. Coffee, and handed out warm smiles like candy on Halloween.

"If you say so." I flipped through the messages. Mother, Mother, Jinx, Connie Jackson, the dentist, Mother, Daisy, Hunter Tafft, Aunt Sis, Mother, Karma, Mother, Mother... "Hunter called?"

She nodded. "Yesterday. When I told him you might not get home from the hospital in time to return his call, he left his home number." Aggie and Hunter had a history. He'd employed her late husband as a private investigator. And it was Hunter who introduced us. "Whatever he needs to tell you, he says it's important."

Keeping Hunter's message in my left hand, I returned the rest to Aggie. "I'll use the phone in the family room."

"More Tab?"

"Please." I walked into the family room (now empty of the furniture Celeste sent—I needed to send Libba that gin), picked up the phone, and dialed.

"Hello."

"Hunter? It's Ellison."

"How's Frances?"

"They may send her home at the first of the week."

"Good news."

I crossed my fingers in hopes that Daddy hired a private nurse. Otherwise, my life might be a living hell. *Ellison, get this, go there, do that.* How long did it take a broken arm and leg to heal? "Good news," I agreed.

"How was Italy?"

"Wonderful wine, food, scenery, and art." He hadn't called to ask about my honeymoon. What did he want? I mouthed *thank you* to Aggie and accepted a fresh glass of Tab.

"Did you visit Venice?" Hunter inquired.

"We did. Bellinis at Harry's, coffee at Caffé Florian, and a gondola ride on the Grand Canal." I was blithering when I should be asking him about Lillith Ames' child.

"It's a magical city."

"Yes." I fiddled with the phone cord and waited.

"Chip Benton found irregularities."

Irregularities? "Who's Chip Benton?"

"An associate at the firm. He's working on Henry's estate."

"What irregularities?" Probating Henry's will was taking forever and irregularities sounded like another delay. I took a restorative sip of Tab.

"It appears Henry hid some assets."

I choked till Tab exited my nose, then I wheezed. "What assets?"

"Are you okay?"

"Fine. What assets?"

"I have a list at the office."

"A list? How many assets?"

"I'd prefer to review the list with you. I can meet at your convenience."

"Today?"

Long seconds passed. "If you like."

I glanced at my watch. One o 'clock. Mother could wait. "An hour?"

"As you wish. I'll see you at two."

Hunter led Anarchy and me into a well-appointed conference room. Leather chairs surrounded an enormous table dotted with heavy crystal ashtrays. A wall of windows offered a view of downtown. The remaining walls were paneled and hung with signed Audubon prints and English hunting scenes.

The air smelled like leather, cigars, and old money.

Hunter led me to a chair, and Anarchy took the seat next to mine. Then Hunter circled the table and sat at a place where a folder waited.

I crossed my ankles, clasped my hands, and asked, "What did Henry hide?"

"Real estate, bank accounts, and a safe deposit box. We're having the box drilled on Monday." Hunter opened the folder, pulled out a sheet of paper, and slid it across the table.

I read. A house in Bermuda. Bermuda? We'd never traveled to Bermuda. At least I hadn't. A house in Telluride. I frowned. A house in Roeland Park? "Roeland Park?" It was a starter neighborhood on the Kansas side.

Hunter nodded.

A sick feeling settled in my stomach. "Have you seen the house?"

"No."

"Is it rented?"

"No."

I knew how Henry used that house. My late husband had bought a love nest, a place to take other women. I should probably feel embarrassed or angry, but all I felt was numb. "How did you find all this?"

"Credit goes to Chip."

Good ole Chip. I studied the paper. After Henry and I discussed divorce, I suspected he'd begun hiding assets. But this? Three residences. Six bank accounts totaling almost half-a-million dollars. A safe deposit box. Lord only knew what it held. "How long?"

"Pardon?"

"How old are the bank accounts? How long did he own the houses?"

Hunter's forehead creased. "I don't know. I'm sorry."

I barked a laugh. Sorry? Three houses. Three. I stared at a painting of a woman on a thoroughbred riding sidesaddle. The horse was jumping a fence (so was the woman). She wore a jaunty top hat and hunting dogs streaked next to her.

"He lied to you," said Hunter.

I shifted my gaze to the man sitting across from me. His mouth turned down and his eyes were gentle.

The last thing I wanted was Hunter's pity.

Anarchy took my hand.

The really last thing I wanted was Anarchy's pity.

I straightened my shoulders. "Henry lied like most people breathe. This is—" I tapped the paper "—nothing new. What do we do now?"

"Chip will handle everything."

Ah, yes. Good ole Chip. "Thank you." Just the idea of dealing with Henry's final mess made me want to curl into a ball and pull the covers over my head.

Next to me, Anarchy shifted in his chair. "I have a question."

Hunter lifted his brows.

"Lillith Ames."

Hunter's face shuttered. "That's not a question."

I turned toward Anarchy. We'd discussed this. Hunter was more likely to answer my question. So why had he asked?

"She had a child," said Anarchy.

Hunter's poker face was epic. He didn't react. "Still not a question."

"Have you found him or her?"

"I can't comment."

"Someone shot at Ellison."

Hunter's gaze shifted to me, and I nodded. "They hit Marjorie."

He winced. "Is she okay?"

"Her arm. She'll be fine."

"Thank God." Hunter stared at Anarchy. "What does a shooting have to do with Lillith Ames?"

"It's possible someone's trying to frame Prudence."

"Whoever it is, it isn't Lillith Ames. She's dead."

"We know," Anarchy replied.

"Wait." I turned in my chair and stared at my husband. "You think Lillith's child is responsible?"

"It's possible."

"I understand why he or she might kill Muriel. The inheritance. But why run into Mother? Why shoot at me?"

"To make Prudence look guilty."

Hunter rubbed his chin. "If Prudence killed her mother, the other heir could contest the will and get everything. Conversely, if the heir killed Muriel, Prudence might claim their share."

Anarchy gave my fingers a gentle squeeze. "It's no secret how Prudence feels about you."

She hated me. I nodded. Slowly. "So Lillith's child kills Muriel, then attacks Mother? How did they get Muriel's car?"

"They stole the keys when they killed Muriel."

"So Prudence was telling the truth."

"Then she disappeared."

"Do you think she's dead?" I asked. Maybe we hadn't yet found her body.

"I think Prudence disappeared on her own. Then the killer targeted you, so I'd look for her."

"That's...diabolical."

Neither man argued.

Hunter rubbed the back of his neck. "I don't have a name. Not yet. But I do have an investigator looking into it." He looked down at the table's glossy surface. "I'll let you know when we have something."

"Thank you," said Anarchy. "Ellison, are you ready?"

I stood. "Thank you, Hunter. For everything."

"My pleasure."

Anarchy and I walked to the car, and he asked, "Where to next?"

"Will you drop me off at the hospital? It's nearly three. Mother will be beside herself."

"I'll come with you."

"You don't need to do that."

"I do. Someone shot at you this morning."

"Strictly speaking, they shot at Marjorie."

"This isn't a joke, Ellison. I need to keep you safe."

The little girl who'd dreamed of a knight in shining armor gave a silent, dreamy sigh. The adult woman who roared (hear me!) clenched her hands into fists and sent the little girl to the corner. "I can take care of myself."

"I know you can. Let me help. Please."

"Anarchy—"

"I'm doing this for me. I'm useless when I worry about you."

My heart fluttered.

Sensing weakness, he flashed me his most melting grin. "Please?"

"Fine," I huffed. "But be warned, Mother's been alone most of the day. She'll be in rare form."

CHAPTER FIFTEEN

*W*hite beach balls floated in the pool. Fairy lights crisscrossed the pool deck. Someone had brought in potted palms, and their fronds rustled in the breeze. A calypso band played hip-swaying music. And the bartenders served fruity drinks garnished with pineapple slices and paper umbrellas.

The women in their late twenties and early thirties wore short skirts that exposed long expanses of smooth, tanned legs. Women older than thirty-five and expectant mothers wore long, gauzy halter dresses that highlighted bronzed shoulders and still firm décolleté.

Most men wore madras or khaki pants, navy blazers, shirts with open collars, loafers without socks, and belts needle-pointed with a combination of their alma maters, fraternities, and monograms. Men who'd ceded complete control to their wives wore Lilly Pulitzer sports jackets, pastel-hued slacks, and bemused expressions.

People chatted and laughed and drank, and I barely suppressed a sigh. We should have stayed home.

The French had an expression— *Tout-Paris*—used to describe

well-dressed, well-connected, well-heeled Parisians, who
believed the world revolved around them. Subtract the Parisian
part, and that's who surrounded the pool. By midnight a drunk
woman would be in the pool, a married couple (not to each
other) would be discovered having sex on the golf course, and
John Steele, a family law attorney, would garner enough new
clients to pay for a European vacation.

When he was alive, Henry loved the pool party. This marked
the first time I'd attended without him. I tugged on Anarchy's
arm and nodded toward a pretty blonde. "Do you remember the
Brandts?"

He followed my gaze. "The couple by the bar?"

"Mhmm. They came to our wedding reception. Liz and
Perry." We walked toward liquid refreshments.

"That's right." Anarchy nodded. "Perry's a music fan. He also
mentioned something about fins and feathers, so I assume he
hunts."

"The Fin and Feather. It's a club near Louisburg. Skeet, fish-
ing, horses, boating, and hunting."

"Sounds nice."

"Nice might not be the right word. But it is fun. Do you
hunt?" I'd never asked.

"Depends."

"On what?"

"The season. What can I get you?" We'd reached the bar.

"Gin and tonic. Two limes." I smiled at Liz Brandt. "You look
gorgeous." She always did. Liz had more style in her little finger
than most women possessed in their whole bodies. Tonight she
wore a one-shouldered Grecian gown in shell-pink silk.

"I'm so glad you're here." Liz kissed the air near my cheek
but gave me a real hug. "I heard about the shooting and worried
you'd stay home."

"Safety in numbers."

Her eyes widened.

Anarchy presented me with my cocktail. "I'm keeping an eye on her. No violence tonight." From his lips to God's ears. "Nice to see you again, Liz."

"Likewise." The smile she offered him was genuine. "How was Italy?"

Anarchy's eyes twinkled. "Ellison showed me every art gallery and museum in the whole country. I had the time of my life."

My heart fluttered.

"Ellison, you look lovely." Perry brushed a kiss across my cheek. "Marriage agrees with you."

I glanced at Anarchy. "It does."

"I was just telling your husband the two of you should shoot skeet with us some Sunday." Perry had a devilish smile. A smile that belonged to an eight-year-old boy awaiting his sister's reaction to the frog he'd slipped down her shirt.

I couldn't help but smile back. "I'd like that. It's been a while."

"Then we need a plan. You girls figure it out."

"Like we want to go stand in a field in the blazing sun? That can wait till fall." Liz turned to me. "I've got a better idea. Ida McBeth is in town next week. Shall we put together a group and go?" Ida McBeth was a Kansas City Jazz singer making her mark in Los Angeles.

I glanced at Anarchy but couldn't tell if he wanted to go. "We'd like that."

"Thursday at Milton's."

"We'll be there."

"I see Susan. She and George love jazz." She tugged on her husband's sleeve. "Let's go ask her about Ida. Ellison, so glad you're here. Anarchy, that goes for you too. We can't wait to catch up on Thursday."

Mother had convinced me Anarchy would never be accepted. That Liz and Perry were going out of their way to welcome him warmed my heart.

When they disappeared into the crowd, I asked, "Will you please excuse me?"

"Where are you going?"

"The powder room."

"I'll escort you."

"I'm fine on my own."

"Someone shot at you this morning."

"We're at the club."

He lifted his left eyebrow but refrained from enumerating the number of times I'd been attacked at the club.

"Fine," I ceded. "But let's go inside. The ladies' room for the pool always smells like chlorine and Coppertone." I didn't mind when I wore a swimsuit, but I had higher standards when I wore Halston. Not my favorite designer, but this dress checked every box. A modest halter that tied behind my neck, an open back, and a breezy skirt that allowed freedom of movement. Plus the color, a burnished bronze, suited me.

"Lead the way."

We slipped through the crowd around the pool and entered the club house.

"The place is empty," he observed.

"Most everyone's at the party."

He captured my hand and pulled me to a stop. Then he kissed me, and I forgot all about the powder room.

When we separated, he whispered, "You look beautiful tonight, Mrs. Jones."

"You're not so bad yourself." He wore khakis, a white linen shirt, and a navy blazer.

"You could at least pretend." The woman's voice was strident. And bitter.

Anarchy and I stilled. We stood in a shadowed alcove near the paneled phone booths.

"Calm down," said a man. I winced for him. Didn't he realize *calm down* ranked among the worst things a man could say to an angry woman?

"I will not calm down! First you cheat on me. Now you ignore me."

Anarchy pulled me into one of the phone booths and reached for the door.

"Don't," I whispered. "If you close the door, the light will turn on."

"You're over-reacting," said the man.

I winced again. Whoever this man was, he didn't understand women. At all. Men didn't have to agree with a woman's feelings, but denigrating her anger or sadness or frustration as being over-emotional was like waving a red cape in front of a bull.

"You looked straight down her dress."

"I did not. You're the only one for me." He sounded sincere.

"Liar," she spat. Apparently she'd heard that line before. "If that were true, you wouldn't have dropped your keys in the fishbowl."

Their voices were growing louder, and I crossed my fingers they didn't see us. This was not a conversation meant for sharing.

"If *she* were here tonight, your keys would still be in your pocket."

"Enough!" he barked.

A couple swept by us. I got a peek of blue blazer, then they were gone.

"Did you recognize them?" Anarchy asked.

"Think you can stop a murder?" The woman had sounded mad enough to stab her husband through the heart.

"Very funny." He kissed my nose.

"They passed us too quickly, and people sound different when they yell. No idea who she was."

"What about him?"

"Nope." I lifted onto my toes and kissed his cheek.

"Fishbowl?"

I shuddered. "I guess so."

"Is that a regular thing?"

"I wouldn't know." Such a lie.

He tilted his head as if he sensed the falseness.

"Okay," I admitted. "I know. But not from personal experience. It's a regular occurrence."

We returned to the party, and Libba found us immediately. "You're here. I thought you'd cancel." Her dress, a high-necked silk jersey print (peach and hot pink orchids played hide-and-seek with palm fronds), was a surprise. It was beautiful. It was modest. Wait. It wasn't modest. It was open at the sides and held together with ties no thicker than angel hair pasta (one at breast level, the other near her hips). No underwear possible. One good yank and a stiff wind, and she'd be completely revealed. "You have an excuse. Two excuses. Frances and Marjorie. Plus, you hate this party."

"Only because Henry loved it." My lack of experience with the fishbowl didn't apply to my late husband.

Libba glanced at Anarchy who was looking anywhere but her dress. "Charlie's at the bar getting me a drink." Libba was never subtle. Not in clothing. Not in hints.

He grinned. "Another gin and tonic, Ellison?"

"Please."

"Be right back."

Libba watched him walk away. "He seems particularly protective."

"He's worried someone will shoot me."

"At the club?" Libba considered her question then chuckled. "He has a point. So, we just got here. Has anyone been caught yet?"

"Caught?"

She waggled her brows.

"Swizzling?"

She laughed, drawing the attention of every man within fifteen feet. *Would the ties hold?* "Swizzling. I like it. Does that mean men have swizzle sticks?"

Trust Libba to go there. Heat warmed my cheeks, which made her laugh harder.

The men held their collective breaths. Would the flimsy ties hold?

"Ellison!" Connie Jackson enveloped me in a highly perfumed one-armed hug. "I heard about Marjorie. How awful. So frightening! I'm so glad you're here."

I extricated myself. "It's always a memorable party."

Connie held one of the fruity drinks, and I thanked my lucky stars she hadn't poured it down my back when she hugged me. She reeked of one too many drinks. As I watched, she sucked through a brightly colored straw. "These are delicious. Have you had one?"

"Not yet." Not ever.

"What happened to Marjorie this morning?" she asked.

"She went outside, and someone called my name. When she turned, whoever called my name shot her."

"I wouldn't think anyone would mistake you two."

I'd been told my whole life that Marjorie was the pretty one. I didn't need Connie's reminder. "The sun wasn't up yet."

"Was it Prudence? The shooter, I mean."

I stared at Connie. Her face was flushed from fruity excess, and rabid curiosity gleamed in her eyes. "Why would you ask that?"

"She most likely killed her mother. Then Muriel's car was used to bash your mother's. She's missing. And you two have never liked each other. Did you find out? Is there a warrant?" She noticed someone over my shoulder, and her eyes widened. "Your husband is here."

"You thought I'd leave him at home?"

"If someone shot at me, Parker wouldn't rest until the person was behind bars."

Since Parker was the CFO for a railroad, I seriously doubted he'd scour the mean streets. "There are other people searching. Anarchy is keeping me safe."

"That's quite a dress, Connie. So unique." Libba didn't mean it as a compliment, but Connie swished her hips, and the panels of turquoise, putty orange, and white (Howard Johnson colors) swirled around her legs

"Thank you. Yours is unique too." The sharpness in Connie's voice made me think she'd heard the slight. Then again, it was possible she meant what she said. Libba's dress was one of a kind.

Anarchy and Charlie joined us, and I accepted the fresh drink. "Anarchy, you've met Connie."

"Of course." He gave her a bland smile. "You look lovely this evening."

"Thank you."

Charlie brushed a kiss across her cheek. "Connie, always a pleasure."

Connie's gaze fixed on my husband. "Ellison was just updating me on the search for Prudence."

My jaw dropped, and I quickly snapped my mouth shut.

"She's proving elusive." He gave her a disarming smile.

Which she ignored. "Is there a warrant for her arrest?" Was Connie trying to supplant Jinx as the town's biggest gossip?

"We have questions." It wasn't really an answer.

Connie shifted her gaze to Charlie. "It's so nice you're back in Kansas City. You and Libba should join Parker and me for dinner sometime soon. How's next Saturday?"

Libba and I exchanged a glance. Connie was trying too hard. Then again, she always did. Living up to Elaine Jackson's standards had to be impossible. Poor woman.

"I'll check my calendar," Libba murmured.

My jaw dropped a second time. Libba was considering Connie's invitation?

Connie turned to me. "You and Anarchy are also invited."

If Anarchy and I didn't have other plans, I'd make some. "With Mother in the hospital and Marjorie shot, it's hard for me to look that far ahead."

She frowned in sympathy. "That's right. Your life is in turmoil." She held up her now empty glass. "I should find Parker. Excuse me."

I watched her walk to the bar, then turned to Libba. "Check your calendar?"

Libba shrugged. "I was being polite. Sadly, Charlie and I are completely booked for the next six months. What do you care? Your life is in turmoil."

"You don't like her?" Charlie frowned.

Libba wrinkled her nose. "I don't dislike her. But she's needy. And competitive. And I bet there are cobras with more empathy."

"It's not entirely her fault," I said.

"Oh, please." Libba rolled her eyes. "There's only so much a woman can blame on her mother-in-law."

Charlie's gaze scanned the crowd till it landed on Connie. "Did you hear what happened to Parker?"

Libba swirled her martini. "What?"

"He went to the Savoy for an appointment, was running late, and threw his keys to the guy at the door. Told him he'd catch him on the way out…"

"And?" Libba sipped her martini.

"That was the last he saw of his Cadillac."

A wicked smile curled Libba's lips. "Parker Jackson has never had good sense."

"You really don't like her," said Charlie.

Libba shrugged. "I guess I don't. Ellison, what are your thoughts?"

I couldn't say anything nice, so I held my tongue. "I feel sorry for her. Her mother-in-law is a challenge."

The man next to me chuckled softly. He knew a thing or two about having a challenging mother-in-law. "Care to dance?"

I looked up into my husband's coffee-brown eyes. "I'd love to."

He led me to the dance floor. And I forgot all about Connie's quest to be the new Jinx. I forgot about guns and murder. I even forgot about Prudence.

With my cheek pressed against Anarchy's chest and his hands at my hips, I lost track of time.

A high-pitched squeal broke the spell. It was quickly followed by a splash.

I tilted my chin till I could see Anarchy's face. "Someone's in the water already?" It wasn't full dark.

He looked over my shoulder at the pool. His eyes widened, and he quickly looked away.

"What?" I turned. "Oh."

Amy Mallard tread water. Naked. She was just back from an extended trip, and the breasts she'd bought on vacation bobbed on top of the water like flotation devices. I checked my watch. "It's barely eight o'clock."

"You expected this?"

"Not skinny-dipping. That doesn't happen every year, but someone always ends up in the pool."

Anarchy grinned at me, and I held his gaze.

There was a second splash.

"Man or woman?" I asked.

"Woman."

"Clothes?"

"No." He shifted his gaze back to me. "It's your friend."

"My friend?"

"Connie."

I turned.

A furious Parker stood at the edge of the pool. "Get out of there."

Connie tread water. Unlike Amy, her breasts didn't float.

"Now," he insisted. "You're making a fool of yourself."

Connie splashed water at him, soaking his khaki pants. How many fruity drinks had she drunk? When Elaine Jackson heard about this stunt, Connie's life would be a living hell.

"Damn it, Connie!"

She disappeared below the water line.

My gaze shifted to Amy who was doing the backstroke as if swimming naked laps was a regular occurrence. I quickly looked away and was perhaps the only one at the party who saw Connie surface near the pool's edge, grab her husband's ankle, and pull.

Parker's arms windmilled, and he hit the water in a Nestea-plunge-worthy splash.

People on the pool deck clapped.

A red-faced Parker surfaced. "That's it! We're going home. Now!"

"What happens at nine o'clock?" asked Anarchy.

A cat fight? The discovery of illicit lovers on the golf course? Swizzling? "We'll have to wait and see."

CHAPTER SIXTEEN

I sat at the kitchen island with only Mr. Coffee for
company. I didn't mind.

You're up early.

"I couldn't sleep."

How can I help?

I held up my mug. "You already have."

You look...pensive.

"It's this Prudence Davies mess. Did she kill her mother? Did
she try to kill mine? Did she shoot Marjorie?"

Motive?

"For her mother? I'd say money, but Prudence was going to
inherit eventually. I don't see the point of killing Muriel now."

She snapped?

"Why now?"

Are there other suspects?

"Prudence has—had—a half-sister. And she had a child."

Does that child inherit?

"Yes, but the question remains. Why kill Muriel now?"

Maybe Prudence needed the money.

I dropped my head to my hands. "Prudence was living with her mother. She was sick of being beholden?" It didn't ring true.

More coffee?

I looked into my empty mug. "Please."

I stood and refilled.

Brnng, brnng.

I glanced at the clock. It was far too early for calls. "It's probably Grace with an excuse for why she can't attend church." She'd spent the night at her friend Debbie's house. "Hello."

"Mrs. Jones?"

"This is she."

"It's Sabra Davidson calling. I hope I'm not disturbing you."

"Not at all. Just drinking coffee."

"I wondered if I might stop by and speak with you."

I frowned. "In regard to what?"

"It's personal. I need your advice."

"My advice about what?"

"If I could explain in person..."

"If you think I can help."

"I do!"

"When would you like to meet?"

"Now?"

Whatever she wanted, she was in a hurry. "Sabra, I'm not dressed, and we're attending services at eleven. Shall we say one o'clock, here at the house?"

She sniffed, and I wondered if she'd been crying. "One o'clock. I'll be there. Thank you."

Someone kissed my shoulder, and I squeaked my surprise. "I'll see you then." I hung up the phone and turned to Anarchy whose bare feet had been silent as he crossed the kitchen. He wore a faded tee-shirt, low-slung pajama pants, and a sleepy smile.

He wrapped his arms around me. "Who was that?"

"Sabra Davidson. She wants to talk to me."

"About?"

"No idea."

"Have I met her?"

"Doubtful. Her mother, Shirley, is a friend of Mother's, but Sabra is in her early twenties. Coffee?"

"Please." He made no move to let me go.

"Mr. Coffee's amazing and multi-talented." Mr. Coffee preened. "But he can't pour."

"Kisses first."

Anarchy kissed me till my knees weakened and my toes curled, then he said, "Good morning."

Rendered mute, I nodded my agreement.

He released me and poured his own coffee. "Newspaper?"

"Still out front. I didn't want to go out and get it."

"Smart. Where's Marjorie?"

"I haven't seen her."

"I'm up." Marjorie's voice reached the kitchen before she did. "How was the party?" The white of her bandage blazed against her navy nightgown.

Would it kill her to wear a robe?

"You should have come."

"I looked like ten-miles of bad road."

"Being shot will do that." Anarchy noted Marjorie's narrowed eyes and backtracked. "Not that you look tired. You look daisy fresh. Lovely." He reached for his collar, realized he still wore the tee-shirt he'd slept in, and shifted his gaze to me, as if I could save him.

"What Anarchy is saying is that you're always beautiful. Being shot lent you a bit of gravitas."

"You're both full of it." Marjorie sank onto the nearest stool. "Coffee?"

"Of course. Cream?"

"Yes." She sounded impatient, as if I weren't pouring fast enough.

I delivered her mug, and she breathed in the aroma, then asked, "Did I miss anything interesting last night?"

"Amy Mallard ended up in the pool."

A single brow rose. "What time?"

"Eight."

"Pfft. That's not even close to the current record at our club. Missy Darlington hit the water at seven-thirty."

"But was she naked?"

"Skinny-dipping at eight?" She raised her mug. "How much did she drink?"

"Plenty."

"I hear a 'but.'"

"She had her boobs done. I can't help but wonder if she wanted to show them off."

"How uncharitable. I like this new side of you. Anyone caught on the golf course?"

"No."

"Disappointing."

"We did hear a couple arguing."

"You don't need to go to a party for that." Her face flushed as if she'd revealed something better kept secret. "What's for breakfast?"

"Aggie spent the night at Mac's, so cereal. Or I can make eggs."

"I've already been shot. Now poison?"

"That's harsh."

"You can't cook."

"I'll make breakfast," said Anarchy. "How do you like your eggs, Marjorie?"

"Scrambled.

"Bacon?"

Max, who'd been lounging on his mat, lifted his head.

I frowned. "Has anyone seen the cat? There's been no wanton destruction since Max and McCallester put Lloyd in the hospital. I'm starting to get worried."

Marjorie, who didn't care about our cat, asked, "What time are we going to the hospital?"

"Sabra Davidson is coming over at one. Two o'clock suit you?"

"Works for me." She stood, yawned, and headed to the back stairs. "Call me when breakfast is ready."

We listened to her footsteps as she climbed the stairs.

"Can I help?" I asked.

"I'd prefer you didn't. Eggs. Bacon. Do you want toast?"

"Please." I settled at the counter and watched the most gorgeous man I'd ever met crack eggs into a glass bowl.

"What?" He waved the whisk at me.

"You." I couldn't help the smile that curled my lips. "You're barefoot in the kitchen."

At precisely one o'clock, I opened the front door to a young woman with a curtain of dark blond hair. She wore a light khaki safari dress and sandals, and clutched her handbag as if she expected it to run away.

Max, who'd joined me in the foyer, stuck his nose in her crotch.

"Forgive him." I grabbed his collar and hauled him backward. "Forgive him. We failed manners at puppy school." The excuse was wearing thin. Max was long past puppyhood. Could I teach an old dog new tricks? Or at least manners. "If you're afraid of dogs, I'll put him in the backyard."

"Afraid? No. He's beautiful."

Max wagged his stubby tail and stared at Sabra with adoring amber eyes.

"Careful," I warned. "Flattery goes straight to his head. Shall we sit in the living room?" I led the way. "What may I offer you to drink?"

"Iced tea?"

"Make yourself comfortable. I'll be right back."

When I returned, I carried a tray holding an ice bucket, a pitcher of tea, fresh lemon wedges, mint, sugar, two glasses, and a plate of cookies.

Max sat at Sabra's feet and hummed his appreciation as she scratched behind his silken ears.

"How do you take it?"

"A slice of lemon."

I served her tea. "Are you enjoying your summer?"

Her eyes filled with tears.

I took that as a no. "How can I help?"

She leaned forward and put her tea on the coffee table. "I need advice."

Max rested his chin or her tanned knee.

"May I count on your discretion?"

"You may."

She stared at my empty fireplace. "I went away to college and met a boy—a man." Her cheeks flushed. "We fell in love, and I got pregnant." She glanced at me.

"I might have heard something."

Bitterness tinged her answering smile. "I bet. When I told Jack I was pregnant, he got down on one knee and asked me to marry him."

"The honorable thing to do."

"It was. And I said yes. We eloped."

"Where?" I'd not heard this part of the story.

"Las Vegas. A quick weekend. He was back at work on Monday, and I was back in class. That was in early December."

She picked up her tea but didn't drink. "I came home at Christmas to tell my parents." She swallowed, and her words dried up.

"You couldn't do it?"

"No. I knew how disappointed they'd be. And my mother started picking at me about the weight I'd gained. And—" she tilted her head and studied the ceiling "—I went back to Florida without telling them." She swirled her tea, and the ice cubes clinked in the glass. "I'm not proud of it. And Jack was hurt. And then someone blabbed. They found out." She returned the tea to the coffee table. "Mother and Dad flew to Florida and confronted me." She took a rasping breath. "It was horrible."

I made a sympathetic noise.

"I tried to explain about Jack, but they packed up my things and took me to a facility for pregnant girls." Her shoulders hunched. "They left me there. No phone. No mail. No way to contact my husband."

My heart ached for her. "Your parents were protecting your reputation. And you."

"I was married," she snapped. Her hands flew to her cheeks. "I'm sorry, Mrs. Jones. That was rude."

I waved away her apology. "Don't give it another thought."

"I had the baby, a daughter, and that's when things went from bad to worse. Mother and Dad wanted me to give her up." She lifted her chin. "I refused, so they brought me and Rainbow home."

"Rainbow," I murmured.

"I came up with a name Mother would hate."

"You succeeded. I wonder how Rainbow will feel about it?"

"Her middle name is Anne. She'll go by Annie. The first chance I got, I called Jack. He came to Kansas City, to the house, and demanded to see us. That meeting was…stressful."

I imagined that was an understatement.

"When Jack left, my father read me the riot act. If I stay with Jack, I'll be disinherited. Cut off." She pressed her palm to her lips and closed her eyes. I don't mind for me, but Rainbow. Annie," she corrected. "I could cost her everything."

She looked at me expectantly.

What did she want me to say?

"Then there's Mother's cancer. Dad says it will kill her if I go back to Florida with Jack."

Oh dear Lord. "How can I help?"

"Tell me what to do."

I stared at her. Gaped. And a sick feeling settled in my stomach. "Sabra." I kept my voice gentle. "Why are you asking me?"

"Because you stood up to your parents and married the man you love."

Our situations were in no way similar, and I was in no way qualified to offer her advice. "Have you told your parents how you feel about Jack?"

"A million times. They don't care. They just wonder out loud how a bartender can support a family." She sniffled. "But Jack's got plans. He's really popular at the bar where he works, and he wants to open a club of his own."

A cynical woman might think hitching his wagon to a rich girl was a good way to bring those plans to fruition. Cynical parents might think the same.

"You should see him with Rainbow. He adores her. He says she has his mother's eyes."

I took a sip of tea and wished I'd opted for something stronger. Like straight gin. "What does his family say?"

"His parents are gone. It's just Jack. What should I do?"

"Sabra, I'm not sure advice from a woman you hardly know—"

"Your mother is scarier than mine."

My mother was scarier than anyone.

"And you stood up to her."

"True. But I wasn't facing financial hardship, and my mother didn't have cancer. What does Jack say?"

"He says to forget the money. That we'll get by. He wants to go back to Florida." She screwed her eyes shut. "If it were just the money, I'd go. But I can't kill my mother. The guilt would destroy any chance Jack and I have at happiness."

What should I do? What should I say? The hands clasped in my lap were white-knuckled.

Brnng, brnng.

I'd never been so grateful for a ringing phone.

Brnng, brnng.

"Do you need to get that?" Sabra asked.

"I'll be fast." I stood.

The ringing stopped.

Drat. I waited three full seconds, hoping the phone would ring again.

When it didn't, I sank back onto the couch. "Sabra, talk to your parents. Talk to Jack. Maybe there's a compromise."

She crossed her arms over her chest and rocked. "That's it?"

"I don't know what else to tell you."

"How did you stand up to your mother?"

"I just did. It helped that I knew exactly what I wanted. Your parents have had a good life. They want the same for you." I held up a finger, cutting off the objection I saw on her lips. "You only get one life. You must choose how you live. Not your parents. Not Jack."

"Not everyone needs a country club and three vacations a year to be happy." She'd held her objection till I'd stopped talking.

"True. Your life. Your choices. When I stood up to my mother, I knew without a shadow of a doubt what I wanted. What do you want?"

"For my daughter to be safe and happy."

"What your parents want for you."

"So you're saying I should send Jack away?"

I held up my hands. "No. Only you can make that decision. Your life. Your choices. Make them count."

Sabra stood. Abruptly. "I should go."

I walked her to the front door. "I'm sorry I'm not more help."

She wiped away a tear. "Thank you for your time."

When she was gone, Max regarded me with judgment-filled eyes.

"What?" I demanded. "I couldn't tell that girl to turn her back on her family. I also couldn't tell her to turn her back on the man who loves her." I was justifying myself to a dog.

A dog who turned his back on me and walked away.

"What if it were Grace?" I called after him.

He kept walking.

CHAPTER SEVENTEEN

"Here's your frosty." I presented Mother with one of Winstead's famous treats.

"Why are you so late?" She didn't bother with *thank you*.

"Sabra Davidson stopped by to see me."

She raised a brow. "Oh?"

"Nothing important."

"Hmph. Rearrange the table so I can eat this." Frosties were consumed with a spoon, and Mother couldn't hold the cup and eat at the same time. "Where's Marjorie?"

"Resting."

Annoyance flashed across her face. "How is she?"

"Tired."

"Hold the cup for me."

I held the cup, and she dipped the spoon.

"Is Greg coming to Kansas City?"

"I don't know."

"Greg should come." She nodded, agreeing with her own well-made point. "Someone shot his wife."

"It's a busy time for the kids. Swim team. Tennis lessons. Golf."

"Oh, please, Ellison. Greg isn't doing those things. The housekeeper keeps the wheels turning when Marjorie's not there."

"There's his work."

"Stop making excuses for him. He owns the company." Her eyes narrowed. "Are they having problems again?"

"I don't know."

Mother put down her spoon. "Did Marjorie go to the club party?"

"She stayed home."

"How was it?"

"As you'd expect." There was a reason Mother and Daddy didn't attend the pool party.

"Some fool woman got drunk and jumped in the pool." It wasn't a question.

"Naked."

Her left eyebrow arched. "I didn't hear that part. Did anyone get caught on the golf course?"

"Not this year."

"Did Anarchy enjoy himself?"

"I believe he did. We made plans to attend an Ida McBeth concert with the Brandts."

Mother couldn't find fault, so she said nothing and picked up her spoon.

I held the cup. "I have a question."

"Oh?"

"What kind of cancer does Shirley Davidson have?"

Mother turned her head toward the window. "Shirley sent the bright pink azalea. Isn't it lovely?"

"Yes."

"My father died shortly after Harrington and I married."

"I know."

She frowned at me. Apparently, I was supposed to listen without comment. "My mother, God rest her soul, was bereft."

I said nothing.

"I'll never forget the first trip I took with your father. He had business in Palm Springs, and I went with him. I planned to stay for a week. Your grandmother didn't want me to go." She tapped the spoon's bowl against her lips, and her eyes gazed into the past. "Your grandfather had been gone two years. I figured she could make it a week without me." Mother sounded defensive.

"I didn't say a word."

"There was a judgment on your face."

"There was not. You were saying..."

"We flew to Los Angeles, then on to Palm Springs. When we arrived at the hotel, there was a message waiting for me. Mother had had a heart attack."

"She did?" I'd never heard this story.

"I looked around that beautiful hotel—it looked like a palace —and kissed your father goodbye. We hired a driver to take me back to Los Angeles, and I caught a plane home. I arrived at the hospital rumpled, exhausted, and worried out of my mind."

"And?"

"Your grandmother was fine. Absolutely fine." Mother's face was hard as stone. "She hadn't had a heart attack."

I remembered our brief, panicked trip to the hospital after Mother's accident—the way my heart lodged in my throat, the way my lungs refused to fully inflate. Mother had endured a full day of gut-wrenching fear for my grandmother. "She lied?"

"Or she worried herself sick."

What did this story mean? "Are you saying Shirley Davidson does not have cancer?"

"I am not." Mother avoided meeting my gaze. "I would never say that."

"Are you saying she does?"

Her gaze slid away from me. "I'm not saying that either."

Not saying anything told me everything. "If Sabra ever finds out her mother faked cancer, it will destroy their relationship."

"Then don't tell her."

Shirley was using a fictitious illness to manipulate her daughter. And Sabra had come to me for advice. She'd bared her soul. Not telling her the truth would be horrible.

"Why did you tell me?"

"I didn't utter a single word."

I tilted my head and crossed my arms.

Mother used her put-upon sigh. "As mothers, we want what's best for our daughters. Shirley is doing what she thinks is best for Sabra."

"But you can't fake cancer. Or at least you shouldn't." The cosmic justice could be deadly.

Mother didn't disagree. Instead, she fiddled with the spoon. "I forgave my mother."

"How long did it take?"

"A decade."

"She ruined a trip. Imagine if she ruined your marriage."

"I'll talk to Shirley."

"When?"

"I'll call her this afternoon."

"Thank you, Mother."

"I'm not so bad."

"You're not bad at all."

"Shh. Don't tell anyone. You'll ruin my reputation. Also, don't think too harshly of Shirley. She's worried about Sabra."

"You worried about me and you didn't fake an illness."

"The child has her whole life ahead of her."

"And I have a foot in the grave?"

"Don't be ridiculous, Ellison. You're old enough to make your own mistakes." That admission cost her. Her hand tightened around the spoon as if it were a knife. "Better Anarchy than have you spend the rest of your life alone."

I sincerely hoped he wasn't waiting for me outside the door. "He makes me happy."

Mother rolled her eyes.

"Daddy makes you happy."

"It's a marriage, not a fairytale."

"Daddy makes you happy." I knew it was true.

"Your father leaves dirty socks on the floor, spends whole weekends on the golf course, and drags me to football games when sane people are curled up by a fire with a hot toddy. I am happy with your father, not because he makes me happy but because I choose to be happy. I choose to focus on his good points and ignore the socks on the floor. And he chooses to be happy with me." She pinned me with a viper's gaze. "You can choose to be happy with Anarchy. But don't give him all the credit for your smiles." Her lips pursed. "You could have chosen Hunter."

Again with Hunter? "That ship has sailed."

She released a put-upon sigh. "Look at Elaine's milksop of a daughter-in-law."

"Connie?"

"I heard what she did last night. That woman is faced with the same problem you had." A husband who couldn't keep his swizzle stick in his pants. "You chose to keep your dignity."

"People deal with pain differently."

"People choose to deal with pain differently." Mother wrinkled her nose as if she'd been served rotting food. "Connie chose to get drunk, take off her clothes, and give her husband a reason to divorce her before their daughter leaves for college."

This was a cosmic joke. The universe saying "gotcha" after I'd lectured Sabra about the importance of choices.

"Our choices define our lives." This from a woman who firmly believed I chose to find bodies.

"Your sister chose to marry a man not good enough for her. She chooses to stay because he's richer than Midas. She could choose to be happy. Instead, she picks at the problems in her life and marriage." She sighed. "He wasn't my first choice, but he doesn't cheat or take her to key parties. He provides. Generously. Women in bad marriages—women like Connie Jackson—would give their eyeteeth for a marriage like that."

I forced a smile. "I doubt Marjorie would appreciate us dissecting her marriage."

"Oh, please. What do you think Marjorie and I talk about when you're not here?"

That was...disturbing. I searched for a new subject. "Did you know Muriel Jarret had a child before Prudence?"

Mother's brows rose.

"She gave her up. Her parents made her." It was impossible not to see the parallels to Sabra.

"Probably why Muriel spent her whole life angry." Mother shook her head. "You want to talk about bad marriages? Muriel and Richard's was the worst. Her parents arranged it."

"Arranged it?"

"Muriel needed a husband. Richard needed a company to run."

"I didn't know."

"There's a reason Prudence is a miserable, awful woman. Why haven't the police found her?"

"No idea. I should get home."

"Already?"

"Yes." I made my escape and found Anarchy outside the door.

He didn't speak till we were in the car. "So, your mother and sister discuss our marriage?"

"You heard that?"

He chuckled.

"At least she realizes you make me happy."

"That is not what she said. You choose to be happy."

"With you."

He flashed me a grin and pulled into the driveway, stopping the car near the front stoop. He was out and opening my door before I'd collected my handbag.

When I stood, he kissed me.

"Marian is probably watching."

"Good."

"Good?" His kisses left me breathless, and my voice was a rasping whisper.

"It will give your mother and sister something to talk about."

"Ellison." Aggie sounded aggrieved.

With regret, I pulled free of Anarchy's embrace and turned toward the stoop where Aggie waited. "Yes?"

"Shirley Davidson has called here six times."

I stared at my housekeeper as my heart hammered in my chest.

"Six times!" Aggie shook her head. "The mouth on that woman."

"She wants me to call her?"

Aggie's hair seemed to spring with extra verve, and her brows rose to the outer reaches of her forehead. "Yes."

I pulled humid air into my lungs and held it there. "Okay." I walked toward the house with the enthusiasm of a prisoner walking to the gallows.

Anarchy took my hand. "How bad can it be?"

"If she thinks I advised her daughter to go back to Florida with the Tiki bartender? Bad." So bad.

"I'll stay with you."

"Thank you."

～

"How dare you?" Shirley Davidson's voice boomed through the phone line in the family room. Loud enough, I held the receiver away from my ear.

As I suspected, she was irate. "What do you mean, Shirley?" I knew. Oh, how I knew.

"You told my daughter to run off with that degenerate."

"I did not."

"You did!"

"I told Sabra she needed to talk to you. And Jack."

Shirley growled. "What business is it of yours?"

"None. That's why the only advice I offered Sabra was to talk to you." I glanced toward Anarchy who gave me an encouraging smile. I closed my eyes and took the plunge. "That was before I knew."

"Knew?"

"You're not sick."

Shirley gasped.

"Tell her," I urged. "Tell her and apologize."

"You don't understand."

"What a mother will do for her daughter? I assure you, I do."

"How did you find out?" All the ire had drained from Shirley's voice. She sounded defeated.

"I suspected."

"And I confirmed."

"Tell Sabra."

"She can't move to Florida. She can't."

"She can. Maybe you should look for a reason Jack should stay here."

"There are no Tiki bars in Kansas City."

She was wrong, but rather than point out her error, I said, "Sabra said he wanted to open his own place. Make that happen."

"I wanted more for Sabra than a bar owner."

I understood. I did. So I held my tongue.

"The day she met Jack Ames—"

"Ames?"

"Yes."

"Jack's last name is Ames?"

Next to me, Anarchy stiffened.

"Yes."

"Do you know his mother's name?"

"She went by Lilly. I imagine that's short for Lillian."

Or Lillith. Was Jack Ames Muriel's missing heir?

"Shirley, I need to go."

"What? We're not done talking."

"For now, we are." I hung up the phone and turned to Anarchy. "You heard?"

"Who's Jack Ames?"

"The father of Sabra Davidson's baby. Her husband." A young man with an excellent motive for murder.

CHAPTER EIGHTEEN

*W*hen I stumbled into the kitchen, Grace was already there. She sat on a stool with the boneless posture unique to tired teenagers.

I reached for Mr. Coffee's pot. "You're up early."

She yawned. "I need to take Ruby and Barr to day-camp before I go to swim practice."

"You're not babysitting today?" Could I be so lucky?

"Nope."

"I need your help."

Her gaze was cautious. "With what?"

"Your granna goes home today, and I've been conscripted to move her belongings."

"But not her?"

With my mug near full, I added cream. "Your grandfather's handling that."

"Where's Anarchy?"

"I think he's found the person who killed Muriel Jarret." The person who'd rammed Mother into the intersection.

"Who?"

"I'll let him tell you after he's made the arrest."

"Is it the same person who shot Aunt Marjorie?"

That was a fly in the ointment. Marjorie said a woman called my name. And Jack Ames wasn't a woman. Maybe he had a high voice? "I don't know. Can I count on your help?"

"Okay." She didn't sound thrilled. The opposite. If her brain was working fast enough to come up with an excuse, she'd have claimed a tennis lesson or a friend in need or a sudden desire to clean her room.

Max nudged me. I scratched behind his ears and frowned. "Have you seen McCallester?"

She looked up from the study of her coffee. "He disappears. I think he has a girlfriend."

"It's not the disappearing I'm worried about."

"They'll get used to each other," she spoke with confidence I did not share. Then she oozed off the stool, slung her purse over her shoulder, and opened the door.

"When will you be back?" I asked.

"An hour."

"We'll be ready."

"We?"

"Your aunt and I." No way was I letting Marjorie weasel out of helping.

She grinned. "You sure about that?" Marjorie was less of an early riser than Grace.

"Positive."

"Hmph." She disappeared out the back door.

I sank onto a stool and groaned.

Why the long face? You haven't found a body since you came home.

"Don't jinx me."

You figured out who killed Muriel.

"I don't feel good about it. Poor Sabra."

Look on the bright side. You're getting along with your sister. This could be a new chapter in your life.

"I feel unsettled."

Anarchy left an hour ago to get an arrest warrant. You're safe.

"Marjorie said she heard a woman."

You know how it is when you're terrified. Maybe she made a mistake. Maybe now she'll be the one who finds bodies.

A woman could hope. "She did say she missed excitement."

There you have it. More coffee?

"Please."

"Who are you talking to?" Marjorie stood at the bottom of the back stairs with a bemused expression on her face.

"Myself."

"As long as no one talks back."

I winked at Mr. Coffee. "You ready for the big day?"

"Big day?"

"Mother goes home."

She leaned against the door frame. "You realize it will be worse. Much worse. Without the nurses to boss around, she'll call us."

"Daddy hired a nurse."

"I give it an hour before Mother runs her off."

"This nurse specializes in cantankerous patients."

Marjorie shook her head at my optimism. "She hasn't met Mother."

"Don't be such a pessimist."

"Don't be such a Pollyanna. Also, if we're going to continue this argument, I need coffee."

I poured her a cup and fetched the cream from the refrigerator.

Marjorie sat at the island, sipped, sighed, then asked, "What exactly are we doing?"

"Going to the hospital, loading up the florist's shop in Mother's room, and taking it to her house."

"That's it?"

"I imagine she'll want us to take the things we brought her."

"Did you hire a moving van?"

"Ha, ha." I swirled the last of the coffee in my cup. "Thank you for coming."

"To the hospital? What else am I going to do?"

"To Kansas City. It helped to have you here."

She stared into her cup for long seconds, then lifted her gaze. "They come once a year. For a week. I love them, but those seven days last an eternity. Mother critiques the house, my clothes, my friends, and how I spend my time. Daddy plays golf with some friend of his. The kids resent missing time with their friends. And Greg senses Mother's disapproval. It's the worst. You get the other fifty-one weeks. Coming when Mother's in the hospital is the least I could do."

I reached for her hand. "I'm glad you're here."

"Me, too."

The hospital loaned us a cart with three shelves. Shelves currently filled with eighteen novels, six potted plants, seven floral arrangements, Mother's stationery, and a cup of pens.

"This will take forever," Grace complained. "We barely made a dent. And Granna's cran-kee. What did you do, Mom?"

Her granna wasn't the only cranky one. "What makes you think it's my fault?"

"Um...the death glare she gave you?"

"Oh. That. I called Shirley Davidson's bluff." And it was possible Shirley accused Mother of tipping me off.

"She's not happy with me either," said Marjorie. *Ellison never gets shot. Why didn't you duck?* As if I'm faster than a bullet."

"Mom ends up here all the time. The ladies in the coffee shop know me by name and always save me the last slice of lemon meringue pie."

"I'm not here that often."

Grace rolled her eyes, and we pushed the cart to the car and unloaded.

"I wish there was a cart at Granna's."

"Just be glad Granna's not at Granna's," said Marjorie. If she were at home, Mother would make unloading the flowers into a major production.

We poured most of the water out of the floral arrangements and loaded the car. Eighteen novels, six potted plants, seven floral arrangements, Mother's stationery, and a cup of pens, plus two women and a teenager made for a tight fit.

When we arrived at Mother and Daddy's, I carried Shirley's azaleas and a Boston fern to the front door and rang the bell.

The housekeeper didn't answer.

Grace, who held three potted orchids, groaned. "Where is she?"

"She's supposed to be here." I jabbed the doorbell a second time.

"Well, she's not. Do you have keys?"

"Marjorie!"

My sister, who carried a single floral arrangement with her good hand, moseyed up the walk. "What's the problem?"

"No one's answering. There are keys in my purse. Can you dig for them?"

She put down the vase and shoved her hand into the bag hanging from my shoulder. "What's this?" She pulled out the folded paper from Hunter's office.

The fern was heavy. "Not keys."

She unfolded the sheet and read. "Ellison, what is this?"

"Part of Henry's estate." I had no desire to tell Grace her father had hidden assets. "Hunter gave me the list a few days ago."

"You have a house in Bermuda?"

"We do?" asked Grace. "When can we go?"

Marjorie frowned. "And a house in Roeland Park."

"The keys?"

"Roeland Park," Marjorie repeated as she dug hard enough to make the strap cut into my shoulder.

How could a fern weigh so much? "Roeland Park. There's nothing special about Roeland Park."

"Got 'em." She lifted the keys in the air like a trophy.

We opened the door, lugged eighteen novels, six potted plants, seven floral arrangements, Mother's stationery, and a cup of pens inside, put fresh water in the vases, then took a breath.

"I want to see the house," said Marjorie.

"Which house?" I frowned at her. She'd been staying at my house. And aside from a new ceiling and chandelier, nothing had changed in Mother and Daddy's house since 1966.

"The house from the list." Her tone suggested I was a few bricks shy of a full load.

"We can't go to Bermuda."

"The house in Roeland Park." There was a hardness around Marjorie's eyes.

"Why?"

"Just curious. Are you in a hurry to get back to the hospital?"

I pictured Mother's furious expression. "Not in the slightest."

"Let's go look at the house," she urged. "It'll take less than twenty minutes."

It wasn't as if I enjoyed death glares. And that was all that waited for me at the hospital. "Fine."

She flashed a triumphant grin.

I stopped the car in front of a small Cape-style house. Its soft yellow paint, navy door and white trim looked... sweet. Sweet and Henry did not go together.

"The curtain moved," said Marjorie.

"It did not."

"It did," said Grace. "I saw it."

"Maybe it's rented," I replied.

"Did Hunter tell you it was rented?"

"No."

"Maybe you've got a squatter," Marjorie suggested.

Then I understood. Henry had a love nest, and Prudence was missing. She might be the squatter. "You think it's Prudence?"

"We'll never know unless we look." Marjorie opened the car door and got out.

"Marjorie!" Had she lost her ever-loving mind? "Prudence may have shot you."

"I heard you and Anarchy talking. It was the Ames boy."

"You said it was a woman!"

"It was early. I was wrong."

"This is reckless."

"Why do you get all the excitement?" She closed the car door and walked toward the house.

I groaned. "Grace, stay in the car."

"But—"

"Stay!"

She crossed her arms, rolled her eyes, and slumped in the back seat. "Fine."

I followed my sister. "This is a terrible idea."

"What's the worst thing that could happen?" Her finger hovered above the doorbell.

"Prudence opens the door and shoots you in the face."

"Don't be ridiculous, Ellison." She sounded exactly like Mother. "Prudence would shoot you." She jabbed the button.

The door cracked, and Prudence peeked out. "What are you doing here?"

"I own this house. What are you doing here?"

She gazed out at the quiet street, then caught her lip in her long teeth. "Get inside."

"Are you planning to shoot us?" asked Marjorie. Did she believe Prudence might give an honest answer?

I wasn't that foolish.

"I won't shoot you."

Marjorie entered the house.

"Marjorie!"

She didn't respond. I hesitated and glanced back at the car where a slumped Grace was invisible in the backseat, then followed my sister.

The front door opened into the living room which held a television, small couch and a coffee table covered with empty coffee mugs, empty wine bottles, and dirty cereal bowls.

"I didn't kill my mother," said Prudence. "Someone else killed her, then they stole her car. They're after me."

Neither Marjorie nor I said a word. We just stared at the horse-toothed woman with messy hair and dirty sweat pants.

"I didn't shove your mother into that intersection. You have to believe me."

"Then why are you hiding?" asked Marjorie.

"Someone's after me."

"Who?"

She shook her head. "I don't know. I have to find them and clear my name."

"It looks to me like you've been watching television," Marjorie observed. It was kind of her not to mention the nine empty wine bottles.

"Only because you—" Prudence pointed at me "—won't tell your husband I'm innocent. So he hasn't been looking for the real killer."

Ah. This was my fault.

"You shot me," said Marjorie.

Prudence's jaw dropped. "What?"

"You waited outside Ellison's house and called her name. When I turned my head, you shot me."

"Why would I wait outside Ellison's house?"

Marjorie surveyed Prudence's mess. "It's not as if you have anything better to do."

Prudence flushed. "I didn't shoot you."

"Then who did?" Marjorie insisted.

Prudence's upper lip curled in a sneer. "How would I know? I bet there are loads of people who'd like to shoot Ellison. Maybe it's the same person who killed my mother."

I counted to ten and scanned the living room. One of my early paintings hung above the small fireplace. "What is this place?"

Prudence's face shuttered.

From the living room, I could see through the dining room into the kitchen. I ignored the sink filled with dirty dishes, the dining table covered in tabloid magazines, and the lingering smell of burnt toast, and made my way to the hall leading to the bedrooms.

"Where do you think you're going?" Prudence demanded.

"To see the rest of the house."

"You have no right!"

"I own this place." I opened the first door and found an unmade double bed and a dresser. Clothes littered the floor, and I smelled Prudence's cloying perfume. I shut the door and walked farther down the hall.

When I opened the next door, the breath whooshed from my lungs. This bedroom was larger. And wasn't a bedroom. One wall was covered with—I squeezed my eyes shut. When I opened them, nothing had changed. I stepped inside—I couldn't help myself—and reached for a whip, the kind used when lunging a horse. It was the only thing hanging on the wall that I recognized.

My husband had created his own sex dungeon. And Prudence Davies still held the keys.

We needed to leave. Now.

My fingers closed around the door handle, and I paused. I heard three voices. Three.

My blood ran cold. The last thing I wanted was for Grace to

discover that her father, who she'd adored, had built a sex dungeon.

I cracked the door.

"Did you think I'd let you take my husband?" It was a woman's voice.

Thank heavens. Whoever was in the living room, it wasn't Grace.

I peeked into the hallway.

I spied Marjorie with her good hand held high in the air. Prudence and the other woman were blocked by the wall.

Marjorie saw me and mouthed "gun."

The woman had a gun?

I glanced over my shoulder at Henry's wall of horrors.

I spotted a bull whip I'd missed the first time I looked. When Marjorie and I were girls and bored out of our minds on visits to our grandparents' farm, we'd learned to crack bull whips. I still had a scar on my thigh from one of Marjorie's cracks. Why had Henry wanted a bull whip? I did my best to erase the answer from my brain and took the whip off the wall.

Then I eased the door open and tiptoed into the hall.

"I know you're here, Ellison."

I recognized the voice and froze. "Connie?" Why did Connie have a gun?

"Come out. Now."

I slipped the bull whip into my waistband near the small of my back, then rounded the corner into the living room. "Connie, what are you doing?"

She pointed a revolver at Prudence. "She's a horrible woman."

"No argument. But you can't kill her."

"I didn't want to. I wanted her to suffer."

"Why?" asked Marjorie.

"She and Parker."

"I get it. When she was with Henry, I wanted to rip out her

fingernails." Not really, but Connie looked like she needed some empathy. "Prudence isn't worth prison." Even as I said the words, I realized my mistake.

Connie had killed Muriel and tried to frame Prudence.

Connie broke her collarbone when she hit mother's car.

Connie shot at me and hit Marjorie.

Anarchy had been right about someone framing Prudence. He'd been wrong about the motive.

"You framed Prudence for her mother's death."

"Shut up, Ellison." Marjorie's voice was squeaky.

"And when that didn't work, you used Muriel's car to ram Mother into an intersection."

"I stole the car keys the night I killed Muriel. Spotting your mother was a happy accident."

"That's how you broke your collar bone."

"Why?" asked Prudence.

"You can't have Parker. Did you think I'd let you have him?"

"You shot me? Marjorie's squeak was outraged.

"I thought Ellison's husband would find Prudence if Ellison was in danger. Instead, he went to a party."

"How did you find me?" Prudence demanded.

"I followed Ellison."

Prudence scowled at me.

Fear tightened my chest. Not because Prudence looked ready to kill me, and not because Connie had a gun. Grace. Was she still in the car? Was she okay?

"When she's gone..." Connie waved the gun wildly.

"Careful where you point that thing." Marjorie's squeak was approaching the level only dogs could hear.

Connie ignored her. "When she's gone, Parker will come to his senses."

I'd seen Parker's expression after Connie pulled him into the pool. If she thought there was a happy ending in their future, she was delusional.

"Well," squeaked Marjorie. "We'll leave you to it." She inched toward the door.

"I can't let you go," said Connie. "If Ellison's husband had done his job, this wouldn't have happened."

"Connie." I tried for a soothing tone.

"Don't *Connie* me. You know exactly what I've endured. She slept with your husband, too. She deserves to be punished."

"Absolutely." Marjorie nodded so hard her teeth probably rattled. "Couldn't agree more. But Ellison and I are innocent."

"You know the truth. I can't let you go." Something in Connie's mind had snapped. There was no other explanation.

I reached for the bull whip.

"I am sorry, Marjorie." Connie shifted her aim. She was going to shoot my sister.

Prudence lunged toward the front door.

Bang!

Prudence crashed to the floor.

The gunshot rang in my ears, and my hand closed around the whip's handle. I could do this.

Connie swung the gun's muzzle toward Marjorie, and I unleashed the whip. Its tip wrapped around Connie's wrist and I yanked. Hard.

Bang!

Marjorie dropped to the floor. Connie's wrist jerked, and the gun fell.

Marjorie, who was bleeding—why was she bleeding?— scrambled for the gun. So did Connie.

I hesitated. Could I help Marjorie, or would I be in the way. Marjorie was motivated, but Connie was crazy.

I shifted my gaze to the woman crawling toward the door. "Prudence!"

She groaned.

"Where's the phone?"

"There isn't one."

Seriously? "Are any of the neighbors at home?"

"How would I know?"

"Go!" Marjorie yelled. "Get help!"

I leaped over Prudence, raced outside, and flung open the car's back door.

Grace's eyes fluttered, and I tossed her the keys. "Go to the nearest service station and call the police!"

"What? Why?" She stared at my hand. "What's with the whip?"

Bang!

Every muscle in my body clenched. "Go! Now!"

Without further questions, she scrambled into the driver's seat, floored the gas pedal, and took off.

I turned toward the house. My sister was in there. I gathered my courage and ran back inside.

CHAPTER NINETEEN

A brilliant scarlet painted the small living room. The artist had used an extra-wide brush. I pushed down a shameful urge to run away and stepped inside.

Prudence had propped herself against a wall, pressing her hands against her bleeding leg.

Marjorie, whose white blouse was now red, sat on the couch with a blank expression on her face and Connie's gun held loosely in her hands.

Connie lay unmoving in a growing pool of blood.

I skirted the crimson lake and sat next to my sister. Gently I took the gun from her hands. "You're bleeding. Where are you hit?"

She didn't answer.

"Marjorie?"

"I want Greg," she whispered. "Tell Greg I need him."

"I will. Where are you hurt?"

"I tore my stitches."

Thank heavens it wasn't worse.

"You left us," Prudence whined.

"I ran outside and told Grace to call the police. Help is on the way."

"One of the neighbors would have called."

"You don't know if they're home. People in this neighborhood have jobs. They don't spend their mornings watching soap operas and spying on their neighbors."

She drew her lips back from her horse teeth in an equine snarl. "You always have to be the hero. If you weren't so stupid to let her follow you, this wouldn't have happened."

"If you didn't sleep with other women's husbands, this wouldn't have happened."

"Can we not fight?" Marjorie's voice was small. "Is she dead?" She nodded at Connie.

I didn't know, and the thought of kneeling in that crimson pool made my hands shake. "I hear sirens."

"Thank heavens," said Marjorie.

I stood and put the gun on the dining room table on top of a tabloid headlined *Burt and Dinah: Who They're Seeing Now.* Then I turned toward the door.

A police officer not much older than Grace stared at the bloodied living room.

"My husband is a homicide detective in Kansas City. Please call him. His name is Anarchy Jones."

The boy blinked.

"She—" I pointed at Connie "—shot her." I pointed at Prudence. "Then she—" I pointed at Marjorie "—shot her." I pointed at Connie. "But that was self-defense. They were struggling for the gun."

The boy's Adam's apple bobbed above his uniform collar. "The gun?"

"The gun." I pointed at the table. "My prints are on it because I took it from Marjorie's hands."

"Who's Marjorie?"

He didn't seem to be following my very simple explanation. I pointed to my sister. "She's Marjorie. Do you have a partner?"

"Is she dead?" Rather than look at Marjorie, the boy's gaze had caught on Connie.

Why did people keep asking me? "I don't know."

"There's a lot of blood." The young officer looked decidedly green.

"Are you going to throw up?" Because vomit was just what the room needed. "If so, go outside."

He took a deep breath (probably not the best idea—the room reeked of gunpowder and blood). He pressed a hand to his mouth.

"Outside." I didn't sound remotely sympathetic. I didn't *feel* remotely sympathetic. If anyone got to throw up, it should be me.

He straightened his shoulders. "I'm fine."

"Mom!" Grace's panicked voice snuck past the rookie blocking the door.

"We're fine, honey." I crouched next to my sister. "What's Greg's office number?"

She mumbled it to me, and I repeated the numbers back to her. I patted her knee. "If I leave, they may not let me back in."

She looked at me with vacant eyes. "Call Greg."

I brushed past the still slightly green youth.

"Where are you going, ma'am?"

"To speak to my daughter." I stepped into the yard.

Grace threw her arms around me and hugged me tight. "I was so worried."

"We're fine. I'm fine. Aunt Marjorie is fine." That was a lot of fines. "But she wants us to call Uncle Greg. Can you do that?"

She nodded.

"Tell him to get on the first plane. Marjorie needs him." I recited his number. "You've got it memorized?"

"Yep." Teenagers could memorize numbers faster than I could add two and two.

"Does Anarchy know?" I glanced back at the house.

"I called him first. He'll be here as fast as he can."

"Thank you. Now, call your uncle."

"On it." She hopped in the car and drove away.

Another police cruiser pulled up, and I waited to see if the men inside were old enough to shave.

Six doors down, a woman with a toddler on her hip stepped onto her front lawn and stared at the growing number of police cars and ambulances.

Thus far, she was the only neighbor to make an appearance. And she was far enough away, she might not have heard the gunshots. If I hadn't sent Grace to call...

But I had.

And the yard now swarmed with police officers and emergency personnel.

I fought through the crowd and approached the house.

An officer in his thirties stopped me. "You can't go in there, ma'am."

"I'm a witness, and my sister is in there."

"Which one is she?"

"The one who's not shot."

He rubbed the back of his neck. "They're all shot."

"Nope. My sister ripped her stitches from when she was shot a few days ago."

He stared at me.

"I think she's in shock."

He gave a short, tilted, dismissive nod that patronized while pretending to agree. "We'll take care of her. You stay put. Let us do our jobs."

So far, ten different men had tromped past me into his crime scene. "Do you think you have too many people in there?"

He frowned at me.

"They might contaminate the evidence."

He scowled at me.

Two emergency workers rolled a gurney through the front door, and I pointed. "She admitted to murder, plus two attempted murders."

The officer's brows rose. "Is that so?" He didn't believe me. What did he think happened in the house? A bridge game gone wrong?

"I'm married to a homicide detective."

"Who'd she kill?" Now he was humoring me.

What could I do? What could I say? I was a woman, and the man in front of me, the man with the badge and the power, refused to take me seriously. "She smothered the other gunshot victim's mother."

"Ellison!"

I turned, spotted Anarchy, and felt the tension in my shoulders ease. "I'm here!"

"Who's that?"

"My husband."

Anarchy strode toward us with his badge clipped to his belt and a thunderous expression on his face. His hands clasped my upper arms. "You're okay?

"Fine." Another fine.

"Marjorie?"

"She shot Connie."

The police officer stiffened.

So did Anarchy. "Connie Jackson?"

"Long story, but yes."

His grip on my arms tightened. "Give me the short version."

"Connie and Marjorie struggled for the gun after Connie shot Prudence."

Grace ran up to us. "Uncle Greg is chartering a plane. He has loads of questions I couldn't answer."

"I have loads of questions," said Anarchy. "And I want answers. Now."

The police officer, whose gaze seemed caught on Anarchy's badge, nodded as if he were finally interested in whatever I might say.

I told them everything.

~

Six hours later, we sat in Mother and Daddy's family room. Well, Mother lounged in a temporary hospital bed. The rest of us—me, Anarchy, Grace, Marjorie, Greg (who clutched his wife's good hand), and Daddy—formed a crescent around her with empty plates on our laps.

"It was nice of Mac to bring dinner." Grace popped the last bite of sandwich in her mouth.

We'd gathered at Mother and Daddy's for dinner, and Mac and Aggie had appeared with a tray of sandwiches, bags of chips, fruit salad, and chocolate brownies.

"It was." How would I ever manage without Aggie?

Mother yawned.

I shifted in my chair. "We should let you get some sleep."

"Oh, no, you don't." Despite two casts and a purple and green face, Mother looked imperious. "Explain."

"Explain?"

"Don't be coy, Ellison. Tell us what happened."

I'd known this was coming, had even planned what to say. I took a breath and began. "Prudence and Parker Jackson carried on an affair, and Connie found out."

Mother wrinkled her nose. "Parker has appalling taste in women."

No one disagreed.

"Connie was understandably furious, and she decided death was too good for Prudence. She snuck into the Jarret house, killed Muriel, and did everything she could to make Prudence look guilty of the murder."

Anarchy took the plate from my lap, put it atop his own, then put them both on the coffee table. "When the police didn't arrest Prudence, Connie escalated."

"She stole Muriel's keys the night of the murder," I explained. "When Prudence wasn't arrested, she stole the car and hit you."

Mother winced.

"She left the car in a place she knew we'd find it and hid chloroform and a rag in the glove box." Anarchy laced his fingers together. "She made a mistake there. We'd determined the killer didn't use chloroform."

A pin drop would have been deafening in the answering silence.

"How do the Davidsons play into this mess?" Mother asked.

"They don't." Anarchy and I exchanged a glance, then I continued. "Jack Ames, Sabra's husband, is Muriel's grandson. He'll inherit a portion of her estate. It looked as if he had a motive for murder."

"When we took him in for questioning, we realized he didn't know about Muriel or the inheritance."

"But Marjorie and I didn't know Jack was innocent. We thought Anarchy had the killer in custody, and we decided to go to Roeland Park."

"Why did you go to Roeland Park?" Mother demanded.

I wished Grace hadn't insisted on coming to this dinner. There were things I'd rather she not hear.

"It was my idea," said Marjorie. She side-eyed Grace. "I was curious."

"It's okay, Aunt Marjorie. I know about Dad and Mrs. Davies."

Mother gasped, but Marjorie merely nodded. "I thought Prudence might be at the house."

"Why would you go there?" Mother still wanted an answer to her entirely reasonable question.

"To find her."

"But why?" Mother insisted.

"Because someone shot me. I knew it was a woman, not Jack Ames, and I was sick of feeling afraid."

No one said a word for long seconds, but Greg, who sat next to Marjorie on a loveseat, rested his hand on her knee.

I cleared my throat. "At any rate, we found Prudence."

"And Connie followed us," Marjorie added.

"How?" asked Daddy

"She was desperate to find Prudence," said Anarchy. "When she saw Ellison and Marjorie leaving your house, she followed them."

"We found Prudence at the house, then I..." Henry's sex dungeon wasn't something I cared to discuss with my parents or daughter. "I stepped into the powder room."

Marjorie's eyes narrowed. "While Ellison was out of the living room, Connie came through the front door. She had a gun and she looked unhinged. I was terrified." She leaned her head against her husband's shoulder, and he wrapped an arm around her shoulders.

"Connie knew I was there and demanded I return to the living room."

"I was sure Connie was going to kill us all. Then Prudence made a break for the front door. Connie shot her, then pointed the gun at me." Marjorie's hand pressed against her chest. "I was sure I was about to die, but Ellison pulled out a bull whip."

"A bull whip?" Mother's brows rose. "Where did you get a bull whip?"

Not from Henry's secret sex dungeon, not with Grace listening. "I found one."

"In the powder room?"

"You remember Henry. He had odd collections." Toby mugs, other people's secrets, sex toys.

"Where were you, Grace?" Mother's disapproval saturated her voice.

"Waiting in the car."

Mother gave a tiny nod then shifted her gaze to Marjorie. "Continue."

"Ellison snapped the whip, and its end wrapped around Connie's wrist. The shot went wide, and Connie dropped the gun."

"Then Marjorie scrambled for it."

"But so did Connie."

"They were rolling on the floor, and I was afraid I'd make things worse." The horrible scene played out against the back of my eyelids. "So I ran outside and told Grace to call the police."

"I told Ellison to do that," said Marjorie.

"I drove to a filling station and called Anarchy."

"While Ellison was outside, I shot Connie in the stomach." Marjorie's face was pale as milk.

"She's in stable condition after surgery," said Anarchy. "She'll go on trial for murder."

Mother shook her head as if we'd disappointed her. "I wish you girls would stay out of trouble."

"Now, Frannie," said Daddy. "They caught the woman who nearly killed you."

"Be that as it may—"

"No, dear, they're heroes. And we're going to send our family home to rest. No scolding. No recriminations. We're just grateful everyone's okay."

I gave Daddy a grateful smile. I couldn't have said it better.

～

The sheets were cool, the pillows were soft, and I was snuggled next to Anarchy. "Can we stay here forever?"

"Forever?"

"No infidelity, no guns, no murder."

"No coffee."

That gave me pause. "We can move Mr. Coffee to the bedside table."

"You'd get bored."

"I'd be in heaven."

A chuckle rumbled through Anarchy's chest. "I heard you directed the police today."

"That boy looked as if he might vomit."

"You told a sergeant there were too many people in his crime scene."

"There were."

He kissed my forehead. "He called you cool under pressure."

Somehow, I doubted that. "How flattering."

"And bossy."

That, I believed. "I get that from Mother."

Another chuckle vibrated through him.

"One good thing happened." I snuggled closer.

"Oh?" he asked.

"Marjorie and Greg. They spent most of the evening gazing into each other's eyes like lovesick teenagers." It wasn't the only good thing. I lifted my head and stared at my husband. "There's also Jack and Sabra." When they learned of their son-in-law's inheritance, the Davidsons' objections had vanished.

"So, two good things."

"What exactly will happen to Connie?"

"She'll be charged with Muriel's murder and with multiple counts of attempted murder."

"But she's crazy."

Anarchy's expression hardened. "She's crazy like a fox. She knew what she was doing."

I didn't argue. Not with his logic, not with his expression. "I feel bad for Laine. I can't imagine how difficult this is for her."

He kissed my forehead. "The corpse is seldom the only victim of a murder."

I snuggled still closer.

"When I got Grace's call, ice ran through my veins." His arms tightened around me.

"I needed you."

He kissed me, and we didn't speak for long minutes.

"You know," he whispered. "It's been almost a month since you found a body."

I pressed my pointer finger against his lips. "Shh. Don't jinx me."

"I don't care if you find a body every day, I'll still adore you."

My heart fluttered. "Two a day?"

"Even then."

I'd married the perfect man.

The Country Club Murders

The Deep End
Guaranteed to Bleed
Clouds in My Coffee
Send in the Clowns
Watching the Detectives
Cold as Ice
Shadow Dancing
Back Stabbers
Telephone Line
Stayin' Alive
Killer Queen
Night Moves
Lyin' Eyes
Evil Woman
Big Shot

The Poppy Fields Adventures

Fields' Guide to Abduction
Fields' Guide to Assassins
Fields' Guide to Voodoo
Fields' Guide to Fog
Fields' Guide to Pharaohs
Fields' Guide to Dirty Money
Fields' Guide to Smuggling

Bayou Series

Bayou Moon
Bayou Nights

Made in the USA
Las Vegas, NV
17 April 2023

70745267R00128